"Oh, for heaven's sake," Deanna muttered.

Exactly how much was she supposed to put up with from this great lout of a stranger with his towering suspicions and nasty temper? "I told them you were in the stable. They could have just come in and got you, but they think it would be more amusing to hide down the road and grab you when you try to escape."

"All right," Nash said, relenting. "You told them nothing. You're a paragon among women, and I should be ashamed of myself for doubting you. How's that?"

Deanna wriggled free and made a great show of rubbing her wrist, which, truth be told, was uninjured. "They won't rest until they find you."

"I've been in tighter spots."

"Just out of idle curiosity, how exactly do you propose to manage?"

Nash's white teeth flashed in the half-light. "Throw myself on your tender mercies?"

Deanna widened her eyes in mock dismay. "In that case, you *are* in trouble."

Dear Reader,

August brings us another batch of great titles!

In *The Seduction of Deanna* by Maura Seger, the next book in the BELLE HAVEN series, Deanna Marlowe is a woman torn between family loyalty and her passion for Edward Nash.

Sir Alexander Sommerville is determined to restore his family's good name, yet the daughter of his worst enemy, Lady Jesselynn, becomes an obstacle to his plans in *Knight's Honor* by Suzanne Barclay, the story of the third Sommerville brother.

Deborah Simmons gives us *Silent Heart,* the story of Dominique Morineau, a woman forced to leave her home in the midst of the French revolution, only to have a silent stranger once more draw her into the fray.

And rounding out this month is *Aurelia* by Andrea Parnell, a swashbuckling adventure of a young woman who enlists the aid of a hardened sea captain to help find her grandfather's pirate treasure.

A month of four rough-and-tumble Westerns is on tap for September. We'll be featuring some of today's hottest authors, including Pat Tracy and Mary McBride, so don't miss a single title. Watch for them wherever Harlequin Historicals are sold.

Sincerely,

Tracy Farrell
Senior Editor

The Seduction of Deanna

MAURA SEGER

Harlequin Books

TORONTO • NEW YORK • LONDON
AMSTERDAM • PARIS • SYDNEY • HAMBURG
STOCKHOLM • ATHENS • TOKYO • MILAN
MADRID • WARSAW • BUDAPEST • AUCKLAND

Harlequin Historicals first edition August 1993

ISBN 0-373-28783-6

THE SEDUCTION OF DEANNA

MAURA SEGER

began writing stories as a child and hasn't stopped since. Her love for history is evident in the many historical romances she has produced throughout her career. But her interests are not confined to the early periods of history. She has also written romances set in the more recent eras of World War II, the sixties and contemporary times.

A full-time writer, Maura experienced her very own romance in her courtship and marriage to her husband, Michael, with whom she lives in Connecticut along with their two children.

To Michael, Katie and Matthew

Prologue

Late April 1781
City of New York

The jail door creaked open. A gust of chill, dank air emerged from behind it. Edward Nash recoiled slightly. The air smelled of dirty straw, unwashed bodies and despair. A big man, tall and lithely built with broad shoulders, he had to bend his head to enter. Even then he only just fit through the narrow doorway.

Pausing, he let his pewter eyes adjust to the dim interior. His dark hair was pulled back neatly in a queue. A midnight blue cloak swirled around him. Beneath it, visible through the opening, he wore snugly fitted buff hued breeches, a high-collared silk shirt, a black velvet waistcoat and high black boots polished to a formidable sheen. A heavy gold insignia ring gleamed on his left hand. He was cleanly shaven, his skin burnished by the sun. Powerfully muscled, graceful in his every movement, he was clearly a man of wealth and power.

A young, rawboned man stood near the door. He was smaller than Edward and narrower through the shoulders. His skin was pockmarked, his teeth either crooked or missing. He wore the uniform of a British regular but only in parts, having left his stock undone and his jacket missing. His breeches were dirty, his boots unpolished, and he needed to shave. With bold insolence, he looked Nash up and down, spit in the straw and said, "Yer late."

Edward's eyebrows rose. After almost five years of war, he was well aware that the endurance of the British forces had been tried to the utmost. It was becoming increasingly difficult to maintain normal discipline. Insolence that would once have been punishable by the lash was now more the rule than the exception. Soldiers, weary of a war that could not be won, dared their superiors to punish them for what were ultimately the failures of the leaders themselves.

He understood the situation well enough and even had a certain sympathy for it, but that didn't mean he had to tolerate this lout. Coldly, he said, "Am I? And who might you be?"

"Regis Fuller, that's who. The warden's gone for his supper. He said you were coming." His lips split in a leer. "For the woman, is it? The rebel bitch Harrow caught. Pretty piece, she is, but I'll wager you already know that."

Nash looked at the man steadily as he considered his alternatives. He could, without much effort, exert the full force of his will and authority, cowing the soldier and verbally beating him into submission. If it came to it, he could administer a physical reminder of exactly why it was unwise to forget one's place. But all that would take time, something he had very little of.

Mindful of that, he turned away and strode toward an iron-bound door he had spotted at the back of the room. Without looking at the man, he said, "Miss Marlowe is ready, is she not?"

The man scurried after him. He caught up as Nash reached the door and twisted the iron ring that secured it. "I don't know if she is or not. All I know is she's supposed to go with you." He grinned again. "Good luck to you, guv. Yer going to be needing it."

The door gave way. Nash passed through it and found himself at one end of a long corridor. Similar iron-bound doors ranked both sides. He knew they secured cells, some holding a dozen or more men, others with solitary occupants. If his information was correct, Deanna was in one of them.

"Show me," he demanded, and this time his tone made clear there would be no further tolerance, no patience, only instant and decisive punishment if his will was brooked in any way.

The man frowned but he was wily enough to know that he had gone as far as he dared. Grudgingly, he brushed past Nash and led the way down the hall. At the far end, he stopped and gestured toward a door. "She's in there."

Nash nodded. He looked straight ahead at the slab of heavy metal. "Open it."

The man complied. Again hinges creaked. Beyond there was only darkness and damp, fetid air. Edward cursed under his breath. He seized a lantern suspended from a hook on the wall and stepped into the cell.

The circle of light illuminated a small space, barely large enough for him to lie down in, not that he had any intention of doing such a thing. Dirty straw was piled up in a heap in one corner. In the straw, barely discernible in the faint light, something moved.

"Deanna?"

A faint moan reached him. He cursed and went quickly toward the sound. Bending down, he reached out a hand.

She recoiled instantly, pressing back against the wall. In a voice slurred by fatigue and painfully faint, she said, "Get away or I'll kill you."

It was a ridiculous threat, but he did not smile. His eyes raked over the slender form before him. The hair he remembered as red gold was dark with dust and grime and hung in matted strands around her shoulders. The gown she wore might once have been blue. In its present condition it was impossible to tell. The sleeves were torn, and he could see bruises on her shoulders. Her eyes were wide and dark with apprehension, yet the fires of defiance still glittered within their forest-green depths. Another livid bruise disfigured her delicate cheek. Her lips, normally soft and full, looked as though they had been badly bitten.

Nash took a deep breath, steeled himself and said, "Get up." Before she could obey, or more likely refuse, he put an arm around her waist and pulled her upright. She swayed on her feet and might have fallen but for his implacable strength.

"Let me go," she said, and curled her hand into a fist, attempting to strike him.

Nash easily evaded the blow. He set the lantern down and scooped her up. Ignoring her struggles—and the widemouthed interest of the warden's helper—he strode from the cell.

"Ye've got to sign for her," the man remembered, almost too late. He came running after Nash, waving a piece of dirty paper he'd dragged from beneath his shirt. "Warden said you must."

Nash muttered under his breath. Without putting Deanna down, and still ignoring her futile struggles, he seized the stump of lead the man held and scrawled his name. The proprieties thus observed, he turned and continued on his way out of the jail.

"Where're ye going?" the man asked, hopping after them.

Nash did not reply. They passed through the entry room and out into the alley that ran in front of the jail. A carriage was waiting. The driver, an older, portly man, glanced down, saw Deanna in Nash's arms and scowled. But he said nothing, nor did he leave his seat as Edward thrust the carriage door open and pushed the unwilling woman inside.

The sudden touch of the carriage seat against her back woke Deanna from her half stupor. This wasn't a dream, it was real. Nash was here, he had taken her, and unless she did something very quickly, he was going to make off with her.

By comparison, the jail albeit hideous, seemed almost a sanctuary. Terror galvanized her. She lashed out, kicking with all her strength, and caught Edward on the shin just as he entered the carriage. The blow was hard enough and sufficiently well aimed to catch him unawares. He cursed but did not withdraw. In a rush, he was beside her on the narrow seat. The carriage door banged closed behind him.

"Stop that," he ordered.

Deanna barely heard him. All her attention was focused on getting away. The carriage seemed suffocatingly small. His presence shut out all the light and air. It was the cell again, but more so. He had her, caught, trapped, like a hunted animal. With him there would not be even the pretense of a trial, or any hope that the British court would give mercy to a woman it might consider young and misguided. With the court she could hope for imprisonment, possibly transportation. There would be a future, a chance.

But with Nash? God help her, there would be only pain. She had been through so much already—betrayal, arrest, interrogation, jail. For days now, she had lived on the edge, fighting fear, resisting panic.

This sudden appearance of the man she feared most in all the world was too much. She simply could not bear it. Without thought, even knowing how easily he could defeat her, she struck out again.

She had the satisfaction, faint though it was, of landing a blow to his jaw before his arms closed like steel bands around her. Still, she struggled, driven by desperation more profound than any she had ever known. Far off, she heard his voice and knew he was trying to talk with her, but beyond the sternness of his tone, she understood nothing. The threat he represented overrode all else.

The carriage had begun to move. He was taking her away. In another moment, she would be beyond help.

With the last of her strength, she wrenched her knee up, slamming it not where she had intended but into his chest. The blow drove the air from him, and for a scant instant caused his grip to lessen.

It was just enough. Deanna tore herself from his grasp and turned frantically to the carriage door. Her fingers fastened on the latch. She managed to push it open. Cool evening air touched her fevered face. She could make out a scattering of lights along the wharves behind the jail.

The horses' hooves clattered over cobblestones still slick from an earlier rain shower. The driver urged them on. At this speed, to jump from the carriage could kill her.

But the alternative?

She inhaled sharply, squeezed her eyes shut and leapt. As she fled, she heard Nash shout her name and felt the brush of his fingers against her waist. The last thought in her mind was a burst of regret for how very different it all might have been. If only it had not begun as it had.

Chapter One

March 1781
Belle Haven

A crack of gray light shone between the trees as Deanna Marlowe stepped quietly from her father's house and walked toward the barn. The day was freshening. A fragrant breeze blew off Long Island Sound, directly south of the house.

Deanna felt a pang of yearning. On days like this, she had loved to take her sketchbook and walk along the beach near Daniels' Neck. There, in the shelter of the boulders that looked as though they had been thrown down by a giant's hand, she had drawn the great variety of birds who came to rest and feed on the land her family had owned for more than a century.

Occasionally she would see a seal, and several times whales had spouted within sight. In the summer, there would be mussels and blueberries to collect, and on the hottest days, refreshing swims. She had grown up with the beach and loved the meeting place of land and sea, but it was many months since she had gone that way.

There was always so much to be done. In the three years since the war began, many of the young men from Belle Haven had gone to fight. There were far fewer available to hire on as farming hands. The older men did all they could but more and more of the labor fell to the women. They were the ones who kept the fields planted, harvested the crops, spun the cloth, cared for the children, tended the animals and kept body and soul together as day crept after day and peace seemed more elusive than ever.

And all the while, they had the British to contend with, for Belle Haven was a garrison town, under the boot of General Tyron. Had it not been for the prestige of Deanna's father, Nathaniel, who was an avowed Tory, soldiers would have been billeted at Daniels' Neck. As it was, they were one of the few families to escape that burden.

Deanna's conscience stirred her, as it always did when she thought of what most of the families of Belle Haven were enduring. She tried not to think about the war or politics. As a dutiful daughter, she knew that her political position should reflect her father's. And yet she could not help thinking that the rebels weren't altogether wrong. The British had mistreated their colonies, imposing harsh taxes and taking other repressive measures. It was only natural for strong, proud people to rebel against such treatment.

Why didn't the King understand? If only he and Parliament had behaved differently, the entire business could have been avoided. But it was too late now for such regrets, too late by far. Too much blood had been shed for compromise. The war would end in victory or defeat, nothing in between.

None of which changed the fact that she had cows to milk. There were four of them in all, far fewer than the herd the Marlowes had kept before the war. Her father's proBritish sentiment had not spared them from all hardship, but at least they were paid for their confiscated livestock. Not so her uncle's family, living to the north on another Marlowe holding.

Duncan Marlowe was the elder son in the family and, by rights, the owner of Daniels' Neck. Yet he had chosen the larger and more fertile property inland for his own, ceding to his younger brother the family's hereditary homestead. Before the war, her uncle and father had been close friends, with the two parts of the family visiting back and forth frequently.

All that had changed when Nathaniel remained loyal to the British while Duncan supported the rebels. Deanna saw her cousins now only when they happened to go into town at the same time. Even then, they did not speak but averted their eyes as though she carried some contaminant they did not wish to touch.

The rift in the family deeply saddened her, but life was not without its brighter side. Privately, she thought she had lived too sheltered and pampered an existence before the war. Her father had taken great pleasure in surrounding his only daughter with every luxury and comfort a wealthy merchant could provide.

He had taken her to England with him the year before the rebellion began and had been delighted by the number of suitors she found there. If he'd had his way, she would have married a wealthy British nobleman and settled down to the life her father envisioned for her.

But something in Deanna rebelled. She wasn't sure exactly why, but she simply didn't feel ready for marriage yet, not even to Charles Peter Harrow, a baronet whom she had met in London. Smiling, she splashed milk into the pail as she considered what Charles would say if he could see her now. Undoubtedly, he would have some witty remark, for he was never at a loss for words. He might even be amused.

She sighed, wondering why she didn't miss him more. He was everything she should want in a husband—handsome, landed, self-assured. Most any young woman would have been delighted to be chosen for his wife, and especially so one from the colonies whose family, though eminently respectable, was not on the level of the Harrows.

Charles, being suitably cautious in his ardor, had expressed the intention to visit the colonies and to call upon her family for purposes of becoming better acquainted. Had it not been for the accursed revolution, he would long since have done so. It was even possible that she would have been several years his wife by now, with a babe dandling on her lap.

The thought made her flush hotly, yet it was not unfounded. Certainly, the letters he had managed to send to her suggested his interest remained intact and perhaps had even grown through the shared experience of separation.

The cow turned her head slightly and looked at Deanna with solemn reproach. Sighing, she brought her mind back to the task at hand. When she finished, she hung the pails from a wooden trestle, slipped it over her shoulders and, going slowly to avoid spills, carried the milk to the cooling shed behind the barn. There it would be churned to make butter and poured into molds for cheese. Nothing was wasted. In times of such austerity, nothing could be.

The shed smelled of fresh straw mingling with the slightly sour tang of curds and the deep, heavy aromas of aging cheese. Deanna lingered a few moments after completing her task. The sun had fully risen and light filled the sky. The beauty of it stood in sharp contrast to the havoc humanity seemed intent on wreaking. Impatiently, she shook her head. It did no good to dwell on such things, especially not when the horses still needed attention.

More than anything else, that the Marlowes still possessed a half dozen good mounts proved how well Nathaniel stood in the favor of the British. Everywhere else, steeds suitable for the battlefield had been confiscated, leaving only broken-down hacks and a handful of mules to struggle with the plows, drag the wagons and provide an occasional ride for the children.

But not here. The horses nickered softly as Deanna opened the high wooden door. She stepped inside and paused for a moment to let her eyes adjust to the dimmer light.

Romany, her favorite gelding, was in the nearest stall. He tossed his head and pawed with his front hooves against the ground. In the next stall down, Fleur, a sweet-tempered mare, did the same.

Deanna frowned. She had grown up with these horses, had known them or their sires and dames all her life. They didn't act like this.

"What's wrong?" she murmured, stroking Romany's velvety nose.

The horse nickered again and thrust his muzzle into the palm of her hand. His big body shook slightly and his eyes rolled.

Deanna's breath caught. The last time she had seen Romany like this was just before a violent spring thunderstorm hit the previous year. Slowly, she withdrew her hand and walked down the rank of horses, pausing to reassure each. They all trusted her but none appeared convinced. Each was clearly nervous.

She stopped in the center of the stable and slowly looked around. Everything appeared exactly as it should be except for the behavior of the horses. That and...

A small pile of hay lay on the floor below the loft. Deanna stared at it. The hay had not been there the previous night when she checked on the horses. It should not have been there.

Beside the hay was a wooden ladder that reached into the loft. Deanna put her foot on the bottom rung. She hesitated. If an animal had gotten into the loft, it might not be pleased to see her. She plucked a shovel from its hook on the wall and continued climbing.

The loft was under the eaves at the back of the stable. It was lit only by the light that could filter in through a few cracks in the planks. The air was heavy with the scent of hay. Several barn swallows nested on the rafters. They fluttered softly, as though sharing the horses' nervousness.

Deanna glanced around. She could see nothing, but she heard... What? A low sound, rhythmic and oddly familiar. It couldn't have come from an animal, unless it happened to...

Snore.

Her hand tightened on the shovel. This could be anyone—a woman, even a child, one of the many people who had lost their homes because of the war. But if it was, why not come to the door and ask for help in the proper way? The Marlowes never refused assistance to anyone. Their generosity was well-known throughout Belle Haven, even if many of their rebel neighbors refused to credit them for it.

Who had come in the dead of night, sneaking past the house to hide in the barn? Who was there still?

Slowly, she crept forward. The loft was so low she had to crouch. Her skirt brushed against the hay, making it rustle. She was almost all the way to the back before she spotted the huddled shape.

A sliver of light shone through the planking, illuminating the face of a sleeping man. He lay on his side, his legs drawn up toward his chest and his arms wrapped around himself. His hair was dark, and his jaw was shadowed by at least a night's growth of beard. As Deanna observed him, she noticed his breathing appeared labored. As well it might be, she realized, if the reddish-brown spots of blood on the hay near him were anything to go by. Caution forgotten, she dropped the shovel and moved forward quickly.

Exhausted as he was, and injured as well, her presence pierced the veil of sleep around him. He woke suddenly, almost violently. Instinctively, he lashed out, clenching her arm.

"Who...?" he murmured in a voice that was deep and rasping.

His grip was painful. Deanna tried to pull away only to discover that she could not. With wisdom she had not known she possessed, she ceased all attempts at a struggle and instead spoke to him slowly and calmly.

"My name is Deanna Marlowe. You're in my family's barn on Daniels' Neck. You must have come here last night."

The man's piercing gray eyes never left her face. He nodded slowly. "Marlowe... I remember now."

"You're injured. I must get you into the house. We have bandages and salves..."

"No! It's too risky. I wouldn't have come here if there were someplace else to go."

The brief effort at speech appeared to sap what little strength he had. His grip eased as his hand fell away.

Deanna didn't move. She remained by his side and looked at him more carefully. He was dressed simply in a cloak of good quality wool, a white lawn shirt undone at the neck and snugly fitted black breeches. The shirt's left sleeve was stained with blood and looked as though it had been pierced by a sword.

"What happened to you?" she asked softly.

The man grimaced. Even wounded, he was ruggedly handsome. His features appeared carved from marble by a master hand, and his body, what she could see of it, was heavily muscled. Her breathing became just slightly labored as she struggled to keep her thoughts on the far more important fact that he was injured and in need.

Also, quite possibly, in danger.

"I was ambushed," he said with a note of disgust that suggested he blamed himself. "A couple of Tyron's men caught me out of town. I was lucky to get away."

Not knowing why she did so, Deanna asked, "Did they . . . ?"

He shot her a hard, assessing look. "No."

She swallowed with difficulty and told herself not to be a fool. They were in the midst of a brutal war. Violence was all around them. Did she expect him not to defend himself?

Then, too, there was the fact that Tyron's men were well known for their brutality. They looted and burned at will, using the slightest infraction as an excuse. In Deanna's mind, they were not honorable soldiers but criminals eager to exploit a tragic situation.

"Why did you come here?" she asked quietly.

"A message . . . your father . . ."

"Duncan?"

"That's right, Duncan Marlowe. I must speak with him."

Deanna sat on her knees. She took a deep breath to steady herself. "You've made a mistake. Duncan is my uncle, he lives several miles to the north."

The man's dark brows drew together. "You said..."

"My name is Marlowe, but my father is Nathaniel, Duncan's brother."

His eyes narrowed. With a speed she would not have thought possible, he sat up. In an instant, a steely arm closed around her throat, pressing her back against him.

Held as she was, she could not see him. But she could feel the deadly strength that threatened to press the life from her. And she could hear, all too clearly, the words he spoke against her ear: "Tory bitch."

Chapter Two

Edward cursed under his breath. Damn the ill luck that had brought him to this place at such a time, wounded and in mortal danger with a Tory woman in his arms. Truly, the gods of fortune were laughing at him.

His mission was vital; he had to reach Duncan Marlowe. But all he had succeeded in doing so far was revealing himself—and Duncan—to a hated Tory. Never mind that the girl was Duncan's niece, that didn't mean she'd have any qualms about betraying him. As for himself, it was a safe wager that she would take pleasure in hastening him to the gallows. Either eventuality was unpleasant, but his mission counted above all. He could not allow it to fail.

His arm, honed by a lifetime of rigorous labor in a variety of activities—some appropriate for a gentleman and some not—flexed against her neck. It was so slender that he could snap it almost without effort. Easy words. He had never killed a woman, had never considered having to do such a thing. Could he manage it?

Coldly, almost experimentally, he tightened his grip further. He felt her stiffen but she made no attempt to struggle. Was she simply too frightened or was it possible that she understood the complete futility of any such effort and preferred not to waste her strength?

With his arm around her throat, her head was pressed against his shoulder. Curious, he glanced down at her face. The light filtering through the stable walls illuminated a profile of shocking beauty and delicacy.

And yet, surely he wasn't mistaken...there was strength in the gently rounded chin, in the perfectly shaped lips, in the eyes half shadowed by the thick fringe of her lashes yet which still met his unflinchingly.

Very softly, for in truth she could hardly speak at all, she said, "You've opened your wound again."

Startled, he looked at his arm. Blood dripped from his arm to hers, staining the fabric of her dress and soaking through it to touch her skin. She had felt his suffering while he had remained unaware of it.

And so she spoke of it, not of her own life, making no plea, only pointing out to him with perfect reasonableness that he was not alone in being endangered.

Nash hesitated. It was only for an instant and almost imperceptible, but it was enough. Deanna bent her arm at the elbow, took as deep a breath as she could manage, and slammed back with all her strength straight into his stomach.

Pain exploded in him, not so much from the blow itself, although that had been surprisingly effective, but from the breach of the fragile understanding they had reached only seconds ago. His shoulder felt as though a red-hot poker had been thrust into it. He groaned and all but doubled over.

Dimly, he expected Deanna to run, and he cursed his inability to stop her. But she did not move. Instead, she remained close at hand, watching him cautiously as she would watch a dangerous animal, but without making any attempt to flee.

When the burning mist of pain had subsided, at least enough for him to breathe again, she said, "You have to trust me. You have no choice."

Nash glared at her. As a child, he had been a small, slightly built boy whose pride drove him to take more than his share of thrashings at the hands of bullies. In his thirteenth year, he had suddenly begun to grow, adding inches and muscles with stunning speed. From that year on, no one had ever beaten him. Yet here he lay, felled by a blow from a woman who by all reason should have been cowering in terror and pleading for her life.

It was a highly unsatisfactory situation. Also a bewildering one. "How the hell did you know to do that?" he demanded as he put his hand over the wound, trying to staunch the bleeding.

Deanna looked straight at his arm and didn't so much as flinch. Coldhearted bitch, he thought, but he couldn't make the words stick. Truth be told, he couldn't seem to catch hold of anything except the fact that she was stunningly beautiful, there before him in the half light of the stable, where her face seemed to waver, coming nearer, fading, nearer...

"Hold on," Deanna said through the fog that seemed suddenly to surround him.

He heard a sound like ripping and opened his eyes enough to see her tearing away the hem of her petticoat.

"It's clean," she murmured as she began to wind the length of white cotton around his shoulder.

Clean...like the scent of a rainwashed summer day when the lavender is in bloom. Like the perfume of her skin... her hair... the coolness of her touch...

The pain eased to a dull ache and with it took the fog that had threatened to engulf him. He lay, alert again, and watched her as she concentrated on her task. Her lips were pressed tightly together and her eyes were shadowed. Perhaps she was not quite so immune as she liked to appear.

The thought gave him some grudging satisfaction but it did nothing to solve his immediate problem. Who exactly was Miss Deanna Marlowe, and could he possibly afford to trust her?

When she was done, she sat on her knees and looked at him. Without preamble, she said, "I'm sorry I hit you, but you left me no choice. You were obviously upset. I had to defend myself."

Since he'd been considering the possibility that he might have to kill her, this seemed a sensible enough position. "How did you?"

The corners of her mouth lifted. "I have three brothers. Unlike some men," she said, shooting him a deliberate glance, "they believe a woman should be able to protect herself."

"Paragons, the bunch of them. I suppose they're off fighting for the Brits." He was being grumpy and he knew it, but like most people, he hated being in the wrong. It wouldn't actually hurt him to go a little easier on her, give her a chance to explain herself. The trouble being, after years of an increasingly horrible war, the more humane aspects of his nature were nearly extinct.

"Charles is farming in northern Connecticut," she said. "John is in France, and Peter—" She broke off and her eyes clouded. "He's disappeared, but I suspect Uncle Duncan knows where he is. Father probably does. He just refuses to talk about it."

Edward's eyebrows rose. A brother fighting for the cause? If so, it might explain her willingness to help him.

"Speaking of your father..." The words came out as little more than a croak.

Deanna frowned. She put a cool, silken hand to his brow. "You're feverish."

"I'm not."

She shrugged. "Have it your way." Quickly she rose, gathering her skirts around her.

His heart tripped. He scowled at her, hating his weakness, hating her seeing it, hating the way she made him feel. "Where are you going?"

At least it came out as a question, not the plaintive *don't go* he had feared he would blurt, like a whining child clinging to its mother's skirts. Damn woman, damn situation, damn, damn...

"I need a few things. It won't take long."

"For what?" he demanded.

"You," she said, and turned on her heel, disappearing down the ladder.

He was left alone.

Chapter Three

Deanna dropped the last three rungs to the ground. She landed on one foot, caught her balance, hiked her skirts up and ran. The last of the morning mist was gone and already the air was growing warm. It would be warm in the barn, too, before very long, worsening the situation of a wounded, fever-ridden man who could not be moved safely until nightfall.

Her mind raced. What exactly did she need and where was it? She had to clean the wound, stop the bleeding, do something about the fever, get water into him, make sure he wasn't hurt in any other way... On and on the list went, but it soothed her. She had been trained for this; she knew what to do. That steadied her and stopped her from thinking—for the time being at least—about the extraordinary feelings the stranger unleashed in her.

She entered the house through the back door, directly into the kitchen. A century ago, it had been the main room, the first one built by her great grandfather, Garrick Marlowe. In front of the door was a large slab of stone sunk into the ground. Engraved on it were the words: Amelia Daniels' House. Garrick had incised those words on the stone when he began what had truly been a labor of love.

In the decades that followed, generation flowed into generation and the house had grown. It encompassed twelve rooms, six on the first floor and an equal number above, all graciously ornamented and furnished.

But Deanna's favorite room was still the kitchen, with its smooth stone floor, big fireplace and exposed rafters from which fragrant flowers and herbs hung. Just behind it, in what had been Amelia's stillroom, she kept her medical supplies. Amelia's healing skills had been passed down in an unbroken line through the women of the family, coming now to rest in Deanna's capable hands.

Or at least she prayed they were capable. In the stillroom, she gathered clean strips of bandage, which she always kept on hand—especially in these times. They went into her basket, along with neatly twisted lengths of gut, a package of needles, salve of sanicle and yarrow to stop bleeding, liquid camphor and, with only the slightest hesitation, a bottle of brandy.

With a quick glance out the window to make sure no one else was about, she left the house and hurried back to the stable. The stranger was just as she had left him, lying on his side in the straw. For a moment, she thought he was asleep, or worse, unconscious. But as she neared, his eyes opened and he looked at her directly.

''You're back.''

Her heart was pounding wildly, from the hurrying, she told herself. Briskly, she knelt beside him and began unpacking her supplies. Without looking at him, she said, "I told you I would be."

"Why?"

Her head shot up. Will-she, nill-she, the full force of his gaze struck her. On a thread of sound, she asked, "What do you mean, why?"

"Why would you come back?" He made a gesture toward the basket. "Why help? I thought you'd run to get your father."

"My father is away in New York," Deanna said. She spoke quietly and with dignity. But, for the briefest moment, she wished that somehow this man would understand how it was for her and why she did the things she did.

What folly such a thought was. Her own family didn't even understand. How could she begin to think that he might?

The stranger's eyes hardened. She had thought them a shade like pewter, but upon reflection she realized they more closely resembled the summer sky blasted by violent thunderheads. They suited him.

"You are alone here?"

"Except for the servants and the hands." In fact, there were only two, and both elderly, but she wasn't about to tell him that. Though weakened, he was still dangerous. Let him think she was protected by an army of loyal retainers.

In the back of her mind, she suspected that it wouldn't have mattered if she were. This stranger who had come so suddenly into her life would still do as he chose.

Deanna began to unwind the bloodied bandage. "What is your name?"

He did not answer right away. Instead, he continued to stare at her in a way that made her stomach quake. Determined not to let him see the effect he had on her, she kept her gaze firmly on his wounded shoulder, which deserved attention. The sword that had slashed him had left a deep and jagged mark. Deanna frowned. Nursing the injury would be no easy matter.

"Nash," the man said finally. "Edward Nash."

"You aren't from around here, are you?" She merely asked the question to distract him as she removed the scissors from her basket and with quick efficiency cut away what was left of his shirt.

Later, there might be an opportunity to admire the broad sweep of his chest, burnished by the sun and lightly dusted by dark whorls of hair. For the moment, she had other concerns.

"I'm from Boston," he said, again grudgingly.

"You don't sound like it."

"All right then, New York."

She moistened a cloth with camphor and laid it lightly on the wound. He flinched and his mouth set in a hard, thin line, holding back a groan. "Better," she said, "but how about Philadelphia?"

His eyes narrowed. Her refusal to take him seriously appeared to irk him. She rather liked that and decided to stick with it. It would help in the difficult moments ahead if he had something to think about other than what she was doing to him.

"I perceive," he said, "that you were much indulged as a child."

"Indeed, what makes you think that?" The camphor had done its work, deadening the sensation around the wound enough for her to proceed.

"You lack the proper decorum for a woman."

Gravely, Deanna nodded. "That is true."

"It doesn't seem to concern you."

"Oddly enough, I manage without it."

The corner of his mouth lifted. For all the beating his iron strength and will had taken, he was not without a sense of humor. He took a deep breath and exhaled slowly.

They looked at each other. Quietly, Deanna said, "The wound cannot heal as it is now. It must be stitched."

Nash spared a single glance for the wound. Grimly, he nodded. His concern seemed more for her than for himself. "Are you sure you're up to this?"

"I have seen worse. Our midwife died two years ago. Since then I have delivered nineteen children. Also, the only physician in these parts is well known to put his political sympathies ahead of his duties. Those not in the good graces of the British stay clear of him."

"And come to you instead?"

She shrugged. "I care not for who a man is or what he does."

He said nothing, but the look he shot her was frankly doubtful. Deanna ignored it. There was nothing more she could say to reassure him. Only her actions would count. She drew the brandy bottle from the basket and uncorked it. "Here."

Nash sighed as he took the bottle. "Is this supposed to inspire confidence?"

"It's supposed to keep you quiet enough to let me work. I cannot hold you down. If you fight, you will hurt us both."

He grimaced but did not dispute her. Taking a long swallow of the brandy, he handed the bottle back. "Sure you don't want one, too?"

The thought was tempting, although Deanna never drank spirits. And this wasn't the time or place to break tradition. Resolutely, she shook her head. "Have another."

"That bad?"

"Just to be on the safe side."

He took the hint and swallowed again, more forcefully. She watched the ripple of muscle along his powerful throat and told herself she was merely observing her patient.

Fortunately, he was very fit. Quite extremely so. His body was honed by hard work and the rigors of wartime. There wasn't an ounce of fat anywhere on the whole, long length of him . . . from the top of the midnight dark hair down the chest ribbed by muscle over his flat abdomen to . . .

Stop! She absolutely could not do this. Her cheeks were flushed and her hands, which she quickly tucked behind her back, were shaking. This was not how a healer behaved. She took a deep breath and expelled the air slowly while she instinctively sought the hidden inner place where healing began. This time, more than ever, it was imperative that she find it. She never had been so distracted by a patient, so conscious of her own vulnerability, so simply and plainly confused.

And yet, amid the confusion, the place was awaiting her like a cool forest glen lit by dappled sunshine and perfumed by the scent of fecund earth. The place at the center of her spirit where there was only stillness and certainty, and the strength she needed to do what must be done.

Her hands touched him lightly, urging him back onto the straw. He went, cautious and watchful but without resistance. The light in her eyes distracted him, made him forget the pain that was coming. The taste of brandy was on his lips, and the scent of woman hovered near, wrapped in silence. For a small space of time, the world seemed to narrow to this single moment in the old barn behind the stone house close by the sea.

She moved deftly and lightly, with merciful speed. He felt the sting of the needle and the tightness of his flesh being drawn together, but it was all as though from a great distance. The light in her held him, the stillness enveloped him. Pain ebbed to a dull throb. He breathed in, wondering suddenly if he had been breathing at all, and stared at her.

She was very pale, so much so that the freckles along the bridge of her nose stood out starkly. A pulse beat in the smooth, white line of her throat. But her hands were steady as she patted the fresh bandage in place. Her voice was strong.

"It should be fine now, but you have to rest. It would be best for you to sleep. After nightfall, we'll see about moving you."

A sudden wave of fatigue washed over him. He fought against it. "Moving where?"

"To Uncle Duncan's. It's the only place I can think of where you'll be safe."

His tongue felt thick, his mouth moving with difficulty. "How far?"

"Several miles, but don't worry, we'll find a way." She touched a hand to his brow. "I'll be back soon. Try to sleep."

He heard the rustle of her skirts as she rose. The hay was very soft. A slight breeze whispered through the cracks in the barn wall. His shoulder throbbed but not greatly. He stirred, finding a more comfortable spot.

It wouldn't hurt to shut his eyes for a few minutes. He'd been on the move for two days. His whole body ached with fatigue. He'd just relax for a little while before he figured out what to do next. It was all well and good for her to talk about getting him to Duncan's but realistically, that was too much to expect. She was handy with a needle, though, he had to admit, and when she touched him . . .

A wave of pure pleasure moved through him. He laughed faintly at his own wayward self. Life stirred in his body again, banishing the death that had ventured nearer than he wanted to believe.

His eyes closed, and he slept.

Chapter Four

"That's fine," Deanna told Old Martha. "I don't think we'll need many more potatoes. Why don't you sit down and rest for a while?"

The woman, now in her seventieth year, eyed Deanna indulgently. Martha had been there all Deanna's life, having come to Belle Haven as a young bondswoman. She stayed on to gain her freedom, marry and raise a family. With her husband dead and her children grown, she had gone to work for the Marlowes, where she had been ever since. It suited her to mother Deanna with a gentle and sensible love, which was always kindly received. Now, age was creeping over her, dulling her perceptions and sapping her strength enough that the thought of rest was tempting. "If you're sure..." she said.

"I am," Deanna told her gently. "You've already done so much. I don't know what I would do without you and Lucas."

Lucas was the only hand still on the farm. He was sixty and had a lame leg, and it took him longer and longer to complete the daily chores. More frustrating for him, there was little he could do to help the rebels he privately supported even though he wasn't absolutely sure freedom for the colonies would make much of a difference to blacks like himself.

"I'll take the beans with me," Martha said. "Least I can do is snap a few while I sit."

Deanna nodded. Usually, Martha would take her basket down to the orchard and settle herself on a bench near one of the apple trees growing heavy with fruit. For a few minutes, she would busy herself with the beans until the combination of a drowsy day and her own fatigue overcame her. Then she would sleep for at least an hour or two.

"That's fine," Deanna said. As casually as she could manage, she asked, "Where's Lucas?"

"Went fishing," Martha replied. "Said he was going to get us a nice couple of trout for supper."

"Sounds perfect. I'll fix them just the way you like."

"Best get those beans done," Martha said, half to herself, as she gathered up her basket. "Beans always sit well with trout." The kitchen half door closed behind her.

Deanna waited through the space of several breaths before she quickly dumped the potatoes into water, checked that they were well covered and wiped her hands. With a last glance to make sure Martha was out of sight, she left the kitchen.

The air in the stable was still and warm. As she crept closer, she could see the stranger, cradled in the hay, sleeping deeply. His breathing was barely perceptible. Some color had returned to his face, but in blotches. She touched a hand to his forehead. His skin was hot and dry, exactly as she had feared.

From her pocket, she drew the small stone jug of tea she had prepared. She lifted his head carefully, holding it in her lap as she urged a few drops of the tea between his lips. He resisted, grimacing at the taste, but she perservered and was rewarded when he swallowed.

The willow in the tea would ease his fever. She had also added raspberry for strength and a dash of calming valerian. All the plants grew near Daniels' Neck, some in the herb garden Amelia Daniels had planted, which had been lovingly tended ever since. With bought medicines harder and harder to come by—and of dubious quality anyway—Deanna had no choice but to rely on what she could prepare herself.

Nash stirred in his sleep. He turned his head slightly so that his face brushed against her bodice. Deanna stiffened. His touch was fleeting and completely unintended, yet her body couldn't help responding. Her face flamed as she felt her nipples harden.

The demands of her life had taken her far from the innocent young girl she might have been. Despite her experience as a healer, she was untried in many ways, namely, as a woman. The sudden rush of desire that surged through her caught her unawares. She trembled, scrambling to her feet.

Nash murmured something she could not make out, then drifted deeper into sleep. Satisfied that she had done all she could for the moment, and convinced it was not prudent to remain, Deanna turned to go. Earlier, she had let the horses out to pasture. The stable was empty as she passed through save for a drowsing cat who looked at her with squinted eyes as she passed by.

Outside in the sun, she paused before deciding what to do next. There were plenty of responsibilities to occupy her time, but only one to occupy her thoughts— the man asleep in the loft. Try though she did, she could not regard him as simply another patient.

The emotions he unleashed were dangerous. She needed a calm head and a steady hand to see them both to safety. But she felt she possessed neither. Her condition improved little as she walked toward the house, having decided that the best cure for her state was to tackle the soap making, which she loathed. She would do an hour's penance melting fat and ash in the big iron kettle. By the time she was done, she ought to have her wayward thoughts well in hand.

Before she could do more than stack kindling under the kettle, her plan was interrupted. A cloud of dust rising beyond the trees caught her eye. She straightened, standing tall and watchful as a party of men emerged on the nearby road.

They came in a narrow line, a solitary rider in front, the rest behind on foot, stoically breathing the dust the war-horse kicked up. Their red coats flashed in the sun. Officer and men alike wore three-cornered hats. Golden epaulettes shone on the shoulders of the front rider. A sword hilt gleamed at his side.

Deanna took a quick, hard breath and summoned her courage. It had been a fortnight and more since any of Tyron's men had ventured out to Daniels' Neck. Knowing her father's sympathies, they had little reason to come near. Yet, here they were, at the worst possible moment, looking too much like a war party in search of trouble and hoping to find it.

The officer was all courtesy as he doffed his hat, offered her a sweeping bow and said, "Good day, Mistress Marlowe. I trust we find you well?"

The smile on her lips was patently false, but the young man was fooled. He saw only a plainly dressed but breathtakingly beautiful young woman who inclined her head graciously.

"You do, indeed, Lieutenant Haverston. I trust you are the same?"

The officer beamed, delighted that she remembered his name. They had met once, about three months before, at a dinner given by General Tyron, which her father insisted Deanna attend. The young lieutenant had been one of many eager to dance attendance on Marlowe's pretty—and presumably Tory—daughter.

"I am in the pink of health, Mistress Marlowe," he assured her. Gallantly, he added, "But never better for being in your charming presence."

Behind him, the men shuffled their feet and rolled their eyes, exasperated by such gallantry but too disciplined to give way to the ribald comments undoubtedly floating through their minds. That, more than anything, was testament to the favor in which Nathaniel stood. Among the rebels and their sympathizers, these men felt free to pillage and loot at will. But to Marlowe's daughter, they would not risk even the smallest insult.

Drawing hope from that knowledge, Deanna gestured toward the well. "Surely your men are thirsty. The water is cool. They are welcome to it."

The lieutenant sighed. He would have liked nothing better than to tarry awhile at Deanna's side, but duty—and more particularly, the harsh authority of General Tyron—called. "Alas, we cannot linger. There are rumors of a rebel agent in these parts. I only stopped by to warn you."

Deanna summoned a doubtful frown. "A rebel, here? Surely that would be the height of foolishness."

Young Haverston smiled tolerantly, very much the man of the world explaining its ways to an innocent and sheltered young woman. "No one has ever accused the rebels of being intelligent. They're nothing more than a mob with delusions of grandeur." On a more somber note, he added, "Unfortunately, they are capable of doing damage. With your father away—I understand he's gone to New York—it might be wise for you to come into town, at least until we can determine that there is no longer any danger."

"How kind," Deanna murmured, thinking furiously of a way to decline what was, unfortunately, a reasonable suggestion under the circumstances without arousing suspicion. "But I have absolute confidence that if there is a rebel in the area, you will deal with him most effectively."

Haverston preened ever so slightly. He was no more immune to flattery than the next young and impressionable officer far from home. In his case, there was also a streak of arrogance that made him particularly susceptible to Deanna's apparent admiration.

"Rest assured, Mistress Marlowe, no quarter will be shown any rebel. This cursed war has gone on far too long. We must demonstrate once and for all that treason brings only death and destruction."

Deanna thought of the burned-out farms, the shattered families, the despair and anguish that stalked every road and lane. "I would say you have already made that quite clear, Lieutenant." Suppressing her anger, she went on swiftly, "But tell me, who is this rebel exactly?"

"I know little about him except that he killed two of our men yesterday. At least, it may have been him. No one around here is trustworthy, yourself exempted, of course."

"Of course," Deanna murmured. She was now anxious for Haverston to be gone. Every moment he lingered increased the possibility that something in her manner would arouse his suspicion.

Fortunately, he seemed able to concentrate on little save the snugness of her bodice. The dress was old, much laundered and shrunken, which she wore only for work. Ordinarily, his attention would have annoyed her, but under the circumstances she could only be grateful that he was not more perceptive.

Mustering a smile, she said, "I do appreciate your stopping by, Lieutenant, but I mustn't keep you from your duties any longer."

"If you are sure, Mistress Marlowe...?"

"Quite."

"I still think you would be better off in town."

"If I see or hear of anything in the least upsetting, I will leave here instantly."

Convinced that he had done his best, and mindful of how Tyron would view any further delay in his mission, Haverston agreed. He roused his men and, with a final flourish of his hat, continued on his way.

When the soldiers were well out of sight and the dust had settled behind them, Deanna's shoulders slumped in relief. That had been very close. If they had come later in the day, asked to rest their horses, gone into the stable... The thought of what would have happened made her stomach turn. She had to reassure herself that the stranger was all right. Quickly, she made her way up to the hayloft.

But when she straightened in the half light and looked around, the loft was empty. Only a depression in the straw and a few rusted spots of blood remained to show that Edward Nash had ever been.

Taken by surprise, she turned toward the ladder to go in search of him. He might be delirious, unaware of where he was or the danger he was in. If he wandered beyond the farm and happened to encounter Haverston and his men...

A steely hand closed on her wrist. She was dragged hard against muscle and sinew, enveloped in unrelenting male strength. His breath, warm and with the scent of brandy, scoured her cheek. Remorselessly, Nash demanded, "What did you tell them?"

Chapter Five

"Oh, for heaven's sake," Deanna muttered. Exactly how much was she supposed to put up with from this great lout of a stranger with his towering suspicions and nasty temper? No matter what she did for him, he seemed determined to think the worst of her. So be it. "I told them you were in the stable," she said from between gritted teeth. "They could have just come in and got you but they thought it would be more amusing to go hide down the road and grab you when you try to escape."

His hold on her loosened slightly. Sounding as though they were standing in a drawing room somewhere chatting politely, he asked, "How old are you?"

She twisted her head around, the better to shoot him a dagger-edged glare. "Twenty-three. Why?"

"And unmarried," he said with satisfaction. "Uncourted, too, I'll bet. You'd scare the very devil off."

"Oh, really?" This didn't seem like the proper time to mention Charles Peter Harrow, baronet and major in His Majesty's loyal army. Better to turn the tables and get a bit of her own back. "Then what are you doing here?"

Abruptly, he laughed. The sound was like deep water running over stone. It sent an unexpected surge of pure pleasure through her. She had to force herself to remember that he was a violent and bad-tempered man, one she was helping only out of simple human kindness. The sooner she saw the back of him, the better.

"All right," he said, relenting, "you told them nothing. You're a paragon among women and I should be ashamed of myself for doubting you. How's that?"

She wiggled free and made a great show of rubbing her wrist, which, truth be told, was uninjured. "They know you're in the area and they think you're responsible for killing two of their men. They won't rest until they find you."

He shrugged dismissively. "I've been in tighter spots."

"Indeed? Tyron has over two hundred men garrisoned here and another five hundred within easy reach. The population has been so terrorized that most people are afraid to lift their heads up for fear of getting them lopped off. You're alone and injured, several miles from where you intended to be. Just out of idle curiosity, how exactly do you propose to manage?"

His white teeth flashed in the half light. "Throw myself on your tender mercies?"

She widened her eyes in mock dismay. "You are in trouble."

"Now wait a minute. You said you'd help me get away after nightfall. I saw the horses in the paddocks. All I need is one."

"I'm not giving you a horse," Deanna said flatly. "I'd never see it again. Besides, if that wound opens, you won't be able to ride."

He took a step closer, towering over her. Their eyes met and held. "I'll ride," he said softly. A slow, lazy smile spread across his burnished features. "You'll be surprised how well."

She blushed without beginning to understand why. Infuriating man. He could turn her emotions upside down without even trying. Five years before, at the start of the war, she would have been completely unable to deal with him. But the years had strengthened and tempered her. Defiantly, she lifted her head. "You'll go in a wagon or you won't go at all."

He scowled, a fearsome sight that would have struck terror into her had she not been so preoccupied with standing up to him. "Why is it better for me to struggle with a wagon rather than a horse?"

"Because I'm driving, that's why. You'll stay out of sight in the back and rest at the same time."

"You're proposing to go with me?" He made it sound outrageous, as though she had suffered some injury to her head and he hadn't realized it until then.

Deanna refused to be discouraged. Stubbornly, she said, "To my uncle's house. I know the way far better than you, and if we're stopped for any reason, I can make some excuse."

"For being on the road late at night and apparently alone?"

"I'll think of something," she insisted. "At any rate, you have no choice. I won't let you go alone."

He opened his mouth to say something, something undoubtedly scathing. She braced herself for whatever it might be, absolutely determined not to give in. But he surprised her. Without warning, he smiled, a wolf's grin that sent a tremor down her spine.

"As you wish," he said, "we'll go together." As though he hadn't a care in the world, he stretched out on the hay, laced his fingers together across his broad chest and closed his eyes.

Dismissed, Deanna went down the ladder muttering to herself about the vagaries of men and the inability of any woman to ever understand them.

The day dragged on. Twice she went to check on Edward, finding him peacefully asleep. His ability to rest so completely despite his wound and the danger that surrounded him amazed her. Once he woke, and she gave him more of the tea. He made a face but drank it willingly enough.

Lucas came back in late afternoon with a brace of trout. Martha, refreshed by her nap, joined them for supper. With Nathaniel away, they ate together at the big oak table in the kitchen.

"Saw some soldiers out today," Lucas mentioned after they had said grace and complimented one another on the food. "Seemed like they were looking for something."

"Trouble," Martha said. "That's all they want. Go about bothering honest people under their own roofs." She sniffed and broke off another piece of the bread she had baked that morning. "Crying shame, if you ask me. A body ought to be secure in their own house."

Lucas smiled. His hair was more white now than black, and his face was deeply seamed, but his eyes were still alight with energy and good humor.

"You're sounding more like a rebel every day," he teased the elderly woman. "That piece of paper they all signed at the start of this had plenty to say about old King George not respecting people's rights. Problem is, he doesn't realize we have any."

"We don't," Deanna said quietly. "At least not so long as this war goes on. All we can hope to do is survive."

Lucas sighed. "That's the truth, sad to say. Too much dying going on. Getting to the point, people forget how to live."

Deanna reached for the stone jug of hard cider she had placed on the table. She filled her friend's cups and added a splash more to her own. Lifting her cup, she said softly, "To peace."

Lucas and Martha drank with her. She filled their cups again but left hers untouched. Although she felt guilty at deceiving them, she was determined to protect them from any knowledge of what she was doing. The deeper they slept, the better.

Dinner ended in a jolly mood. Deanna assured Martha that she didn't mind clearing up by herself. "You're a good girl," the older woman said, patting her on the cheek. "But then you always were." She took a candle and made her way slowly but steadily up the stairs to bed.

Lucas lingered a little longer. There was a watchful air about him. Quietly, he asked, "Anything happen today while I was fishing?"

Deanna wiped her hands on a length of toweling and hung it over a wooden pole near the stone basin. "Those British soldiers stopped for a few minutes but they went on readily enough."

"And why shouldn't they? This is Nathaniel Marlowe's place and everyone knows he's a good King's man."

"He believes in loyalty," Deanna said softly. "Without it, he fears we will slip into chaos."

"That's possible," Lucas agreed. The prospect didn't seem to worry him as much as it did Deanna's father. But then society had arranged itself in such a way that Lucas had far less to lose.

He stood beside the door, half open to the balmy night. A few stars flickered between the overhanging branches of the trees. Lucas could name the stars in a language he alone spoke, having learned it from his father long ago. So, too, could he move like a wraith through the darkness, vanishing in the blink of an eye with a skill any Pequot or Mohawk would have envied. He had spent his life with plow and hoe, but there was an air of the warrior about him that made him keen-eyed and unflappable. He put his hand to the latch but hesitated. "If you need anything..."

Deanna turned and met his gaze. For an instant she was tempted, but then she remembered his age and the special, terrible vulnerability he withstood simply because of his race.

"I'm fine," she said, so firmly that he was left with no choice but to believe it. He nodded and went out into the night, closing the door gently behind him.

She waited, counting minutes. Five, ten, fifteen. A light flickered in Lucas's cabin beyond the trees. Sometimes he stayed up late carving delicate wooden figures by lantern glow.

Not tonight, she prayed silently. Let the hard cider and the long day combine to send him into restful sleep. Let oblivion wrap around Daniels' Neck as thoroughly as the darkness did.

The light dimmed, faded into nothingness. Quickly, she went to the high carved chest beside one wall and drew out paper, pen and ink. Martha could read a little, Lucas more than that. They would understand her well enough.

"I have gone to visit Uncle Duncan," she wrote. "Don't worry, everything will be fine."

Deanna knew they would sense then that everything was not fine, but they would wait, giving her time to return, before raising any hue and cry. The ink sanded, she laid the paper in the center of the table. All her preparations were made. Now there was nothing left to do but act.

Chapter Six

Nash was awake and waiting for her. He declined her help getting down the ladder despite the pain that caused a white line to form around his mouth from clenching his jaw. She judged that the camphor she had applied to deaden the pain and the medication she had administered since were wearing off, and tried to convince him to take more.

"No," he said, the single syllable cutting off all discussion. Stubbornly, he insisted on helping her harness the horse and wagon. They worked quickly and silently.

A full moon rode in the cloudless sky. It would light their way but it would also leave them completely exposed in the war-torn land.

"There are blankets in the back," Deanna said. "I've tried to make it as comfortable as possible." She was thinking of his shoulder and the painful battering it would take as the wagon moved over roads rutted from the spring rains and summer mud.

Nash shrugged. He bent over to pick up something he had left in the shadows beside the stable door. When he straightened again, he was buckling a sword belt around his narrow hips.

Deanna gaped. The injured, feverish man she had tended throughout the endless day stood before her, armed for battle. Besides the sword, a musket was slung over his uninjured shoulder and a knife gleamed from a leather sheath around his thigh. A powder horn and a sack of deadly shot hung from his belt. If she had any doubts at all about his warrior nature, they vanished at that instant.

Nash spared a small smile for her obvious confusion as he swung lightly up into the seat. "I'll drive," he said and reached for the reins.

"Like hell," Deanna replied.

He froze and looked at her in shock. Clearly, his opinion of her had not yet sunk to such a level that he could anticipate such language from her. While he was still grappling with her utter lack of ladylike demeanor, she climbed onto the seat, took the reins from him and slapped them lightly across the horses' backs.

The grays were well schooled and long accustomed to her touch. They responded instantly, setting off down the road at a slow, steady pace.

"It makes no sense for you to drive," Deanna said, not daring to look at the silent man at her side who was still staring at her. "You don't know the horses or the route, and besides, if we run into trouble, I'm sure you'll want to have your hands free."

"I don't think you really want to talk about what I'd like to do with my hands right about now," Nash muttered. "Did your father never discipline you at all?"

"He took my favorite pony away one time for an entire week."

Nash shook his head in mock astonishment. "What heinous crime could you have committed to warrant such punishment?"

Deanna was loath to tell him, but neither was she eager to provoke him any further. Reluctantly, she said, "He caught me sneaking out of the house at night and said it had to stop."

Slashing black eyebrows shot up. "How intolerant of him. He actually objected to his daughter going off at night on her own? Who were you meeting?"

"No one. I was only eight at the time."

Nash frowned. "Why did an eight-year old want to wander around alone at night?"

"I just liked it," she admitted, feeling embarrassed. At the time, she hadn't thought much about it except to resent her father's dictate. But now she supposed it did sound strange. A little feebly, she said, "I always stayed on our own land." She did not add that she had gone in search of night-blooming flowers and rare herbs, or that she had loved the night, feeling perfectly safe and never encountering the least bit of trouble.

He thought badly enough of her already. There was no point in raising the dark, writhing word her father had thrown at her in the instant before he wrapped his arms around her in a fiercely protective bear hug. She was not a witch, had never been, never would be. In these enlightened days, who even believed in such things?

All she did was follow the old ways laid down by Amelia Daniels and honored since by the women of her family. If the men in her family found that difficult to understand, there was no reason to trouble them with it.

Deanna noticed Nash shift in his seat. She knew his shoulder must be hurting him but did not mention it. There was no point, he would only snap at her again and deny any need for help. None the less, there was something comforting about having him beside her. Maddening man that he was, she felt oddly safe with him.

Her shoulders were stiff. She flexed them surreptitiously and urged the horses on. It was a good seven miles to her uncle's farm in the back country north of Belle Haven. The town was gradually spreading out in his direction, although now there were only a few isolated holdings perched along the narrow dirt road that had been a Pequot hunting track. Much of the primeval forest remained, pressing in close against both sides of the road in places before suddenly falling away to reveal cultivated fields and land cleared for pasture. Above it all, the moon shone, casting a ribbon of silver light over the slumbering land.

Deanna's fingers loosened on the reins. She was very tired. The day had been long and fraught with danger. She felt drained of all strength just when she needed it most. Several times, she sat up suddenly only to slowly slump down again as exhaustion claimed her. This time, her head, brightly silvered in the moonlight, fell forward.

Nash sighed as he took the reins. He would have argued more with her to begin with but he'd presumed it was only a matter of time before the trials of the day took their toll. She was a woman, after all, and a young one at that, not hardened to the rigors of life or inured to physical needs as he was. All things considered, it was surprising she had held up as long as she did. Now, she resembled nothing so much as a bedraggled doll bouncing along with every jolt of the wagon and in danger of being toppled over.

He shook his head at the thought of stubborn females who didn't have enough sense to stay home where they belonged. He reluctantly put an arm around her, drawing her against the shelter of his body. She made a low sound deep in her throat and snuggled closer.

Nash grimaced. He forgot the throbbing in his shoulder, the ever present sense of peril, everything except the woman who leaned so trustingly against him. Her hair smelled of honeysuckle and lavender, her skin felt soft and warm. It took very little effort to imagine what it would be like to drive the wagon into the forest, take her in his arms and forget that the rest of the world existed.

Until, of course, she objected. There was passion in her, he had seen it in the gleam of her eyes, the stubborn tilt of her chin, the proud carriage of her body.

But there was also fierce pride and courage, which would make her no easy tumble for any man.

Tempted though she might be—he was confident enough of his own abilities with the opposite sex to give himself that much—there could be only one end to such an encounter. She would protest and he would stop, for the idea of forcing any woman was repellent to him. Far better to let her sleep and continue on their way. The sooner he reached Duncan Marlowe's, the sooner he could set his mind once again on the life and death struggle called war coming at last to its bloody conclusion.

But first they had to negotiate the forest track. Up ahead, it divided, one fork going west, the other continuing north. Nash stopped. He knew the approximate location of Duncan Marlowe's farm but obviously he didn't know it well enough or he wouldn't have made the mistake that landed him in Nathaniel's stable.

The horses stood patiently as he pondered the situation. The wagon no longer creaked, the harnesses did not jangle. There were only the night sounds of the woods, small animals and insects, the flutter of a predator's wings...and something more, still faint and far off but coming closer, borne on the night wind. Men's voices.

Cursing, he stood, sliding Deanna down on the seat behind him, and slapped the reins hard. The horses started—not used to such treatment—but they calmed quickly and moved at a brisk pace off the track into the concealment of the trees.

The sudden movement jostled Deanna from sleep. She woke and sat up, holding onto the seat to keep her balance. "What . . . ?"

"Quiet," Nash said tensely. "Someone's coming."

She said nothing and moved with silent agility from the wagon to stand before the horses, soothing them with a touch. They shied slightly, nervous in the night and the sudden sense of danger, but not by so much as the flick of a tail did they betray their presence.

Nash gestured to her to stay where she was and moved forward, staying in the shadows of the trees, until he could see the road. Nothing moved along it, nor could he hear anything. He almost believed that he had imagined the voices until, after the space of several minutes, he heard them again.

The sounds were louder and closer, hearty in their tone and interspersed with laughter. The men, whoever they were, weren't making any attempt to conceal their presence. On the contrary, they seemed determined to announce it.

Nash shifted the musket from his shoulder. He took a measure of shot from the pouch at his waist and poured it into the barrel. He came upon Deanna so silently that she was not aware of him until he was standing almost directly beside her.

She jumped, her face whitening. Tensely, she whispered, "What is it?"

He held out the musket. "Do you know how to use this?"

She nodded, her eyes never leaving him. "Why?"

"There are six men, maybe more. They sound drunk."

"Renegades?"

"Most likely. Are there many around here?"

"Too many. They travel in packs like animals. Some claim allegiance to the rebels, others call themselves Tories. It doesn't matter, they're all the same. For them, the war's just an excuse to commit crimes that would have gotten them hung a few years ago."

His eyes darkened. It was as he had thought. Not a party of friends returning late from some innocent excursion, but men who saw the present turmoil as an excuse to let loose the darkest sides of their natures. Without further delay, he took the musket and the shot and powder from his belt and handed them to her.

"What about you?" she asked.

Nash smiled grimly. He gestured to his sword and the knife strapped to his thigh. "I do better with these anyway."

She slipped the musket onto her shoulder. The way she handled the weapon reassured him. She had told the truth. At some point in her life, Deanna Marlowe had learned to wield a gun.

"Who taught you?" he asked.

"My brother Peter."

"The one who's disappeared?"

Deanna nodded. "My aim is true but I've never actually shot at anything except a rock or a piece of wood."

He put his hands on her shoulders and turned her so that she had no choice but to look directly at him. ''You'll do what you have to, understood? With a bit of luck, they'll never notice us. But if worse comes to worst and one of them gets past me, I'll be counting on you to stop him. Don't let me down.''

Deanna swallowed convulsively. Nash squeezed her shoulders once before releasing her. As silently as he had come, he disappeared into the surrounding forest.

She waited, her hand gripping the musket, barely breathing. In the stillness of the night, the men's voices rang ever more loudly. Nash was right, they did sound drunk, and all the more dangerous for it. A tremor ran down her back. She murmured again to the horses and swiftly took their reins, tying them to a nearby tree.

Her heart beat painfully. Hardly breathing, she crouched behind the wagon and waited.

Chapter Seven

Behind a tree near the road, Nash waited. He told himself the odds were overwhelming that the men would never notice them. They would go on their way without trouble. But the prickling at the back of his neck and the sudden tightness in his stomach said otherwise. Through long experience, he knew to trust those warnings of impending danger.

Still, he hoped his intuition was wrong, not so much for himself, for he had been in so many battles and skirmishes that one more seemed hardly to matter, but for her. Never before had he faced such a situation with a woman in his care. He felt the burden of that keenly. The thought of Deanna falling into the hands of such men sent a red mist roiling through his mind. His hand closed around the knife strapped to his thigh. Eyes on the road, he eased the blade from its sheath.

They came around a bend in the road, six as he had guessed, poorly mounted on horses that looked tired and ill cared for. Several of the men were listing in their saddles. They wore an odd assortment of clothes, likely the fruit of their pillaging. A bottle was being passed back and forth.

One of them struck up a drinking song, loudly and off key. The others took it up. Nash waited grimly, counting the moments. They passed directly in front of him and continued farther down the road. Ahead lay another bend that would take them quickly out of sight. He had just begun to believe there would be no trouble when one of the men suddenly drew rein.

"Got to piss," he said, his voice slurred. Awkwardly, he lowered himself out of the saddle.

The other way, Nash thought. Go the other way, you stupid lout. But the man turned so that his grizzled face was visible and began fumbling with his clothes.

Several of the other men decided that seemed like a good idea and also dismounted. The rest continued passing the bottle around. Nash shook his head in disgust.

Those who were on foot fumbled with their clothes and turned to remount. It was almost over. In another moment they would be gone.

A high, piercing shriek tore a rent in the night. The men jumped, whirling in the direction from which it had come.

"What's that?"

"Over there!"

"Sounds like a horse."

"Something spooked it."

"Let's go!"

Scenting prey, they kicked their animals into a rough and tumble rush off the track and into the forest, straight toward where Deanna was hiding.

Nash cursed. He had no idea what had set the horse off, but there was no doubt what the result would be unless he acted with utmost speed.

Running flat out, he caught up with the men and hurled himself at the nearest rider. Coming from the shadows without warning, he took them by surprise. The first man was on the ground, stunned into unconsciousness, before he had a chance to realize what was happening.

The others would not be so easy. Crude, undisciplined men that they were, they were five to his one. And they were no strangers to dirty fighting. Nash sideswiped a blow from an ax that would have killed him, yanked another man from his saddle as he was trying to load a musket, and only just managed to avoid being trampled by a cursing, wild eyed brute who galloped straight at him.

This last man drew a sword, and, brandishing it over his head, tried again to ram Nash. His maddened horse reared, hooves flashing in the moonlight, missing Nash's head by inches.

Two of the men lay on the ground, alive but unmoving. The other three were in disarray, unsure how many attackers there were and disoriented by the surrounding woods. The wild-eyed sword wielder was made of sterner stuff. He curled his lips to expose blackened teeth, stood straight up in his saddle and charged Nash again.

Nash dodged this way and that, knife drawn. He was by far the better fighter, vastly more experienced, honed for battle and relentless. All he needed was a single opening to get the knife in and end the contest. Sooner or later, the horse would rear in the right direction and he would strike.

It had rained the day before. The forest floor was still moist and slippery. Before he could find the chance he needed, his foot slipped on the wet ground and he lost his balance. The renegade moved in for the kill. Nash rolled, trying to put distance between himself and the sword's lethal steel. His body slammed into a boulder, momentarily blocking all escape.

The sword started downward. To Edward, it sang through the night air of death and destroyed hopes, of life thrown away in a forest glen and of bitter, savage regret when he thought what would surely be his last thought ever—beautiful, helpless Deanna.

A shot rang out. It sundered the night, sending flocks of startled birds whirling frantically into the sky. The renegade paused, frozen in surprise, staring down at the red stain that blossomed suddenly across his chest.

Twenty feet away, Deanna lowered the musket. She stood motionless, white and gleaming in the moonlight, less a mortal woman at that moment than a woman of dreams. Or so it seemed to Nash, who stumbled to his feet as the man who would have killed him toppled slowly from his saddle.

The others fled. The clamour of their flight echoed through the arching branches, then died away.

A breathless hush settled over the glen.

Chapter Eight

Deanna bent slightly and leaned the musket against a nearby tree. If she moved too quickly, she feared she would shatter. A blessed sense of unreality settled over her. She felt like a spectator staring down at a scene fascinating in its horror. Except she was there in the middle of it, her shoulder still stinging from the recoil of the gun and a man lying dead at her hands.

Her knees wobbled. She reached out for the tree, but before she could try to grab hold of it, Nash was there. He caught her around the waist just as she began to fall and lifted her high against the solid wall of his chest.

Swiftly, he carried her from the glen to where she had hidden with the horses. They were still there, tied to a tree, looking frightened but not about to bolt. While he felt a fleeting sense of relief at that, all his attention was focused on the pale, still woman in his arms.

Gently, he lowered her onto the moss draped ground. Her eyes were shut. Not a breath of color shone in her translucent skin. She could have been carved from marble. Had she fainted? The thought was oddly terrifying. She was such an indomitable woman, so stubbornly courageous, maddening in her insistence on standing up to him and irritating to the extreme—absolutely the wrong woman in the wrong place at the wrong time. Utterly, totally wrong.

Sweet heaven, he had to remember that. She was the worst thing for him, the absolute worst. Get to Duncan's, thank her for saving his life—possibly twice— give her a quick pat on the head and be done with it. His hands were shaking and his breath was ragged. It was all he could do to keep from roaring in anger that she was here, unconscious and in danger, and he was seemingly helpless to do anything about it.

Her eyelids fluttered. He stared, caught in a moonlit web as they lifted. Dark, gold-sharded green light held the mysteries of her soul.

"Nash..."

Her voice was a breath on the wind. She raised her hand, pale and absurdly delicate, and lightly—so lightly—touched his cheek. "Don't cry," she said.

Only then did he feel the hot tears trickling down his cheeks. They stunned him. He didn't cry, hadn't since he was a very small child. But now? Here? With her? God in heaven, what was happening to him?

He had faced death before, often enough that he did not find it a stranger. It wasn't that. What had shaken him to the very core of his being were his feelings for her, the desperate, tearing need to protect her combined with the uncontrollable drive to possess her fiercely.

She shifted slightly in his arms. He felt the warm strength and slender grace of her body. Her eyes were wide, filled with questions. Her lips parted.

He bent his head, dark against the silvered glow of the moonlight. The scents of moss and trampled grass mingled with the perfume of her skin. She did not move but remained quiet in his arms, waiting.

Her mouth was impossibly soft. He melted into it, trying so hard to go slowly and finding that he could not. All the passions of the bloody, beautiful day abruptly snapped inside him. With a low groan, he lifted her closer. His tongue plunged deeply, stroking and tasting. Distantly, he heard her moan but the small, female sound only drove him on.

His big, callused hand slid down her back to cup her buttocks through the thin cotton dress. Slowly, he pressed, released, pressed again in the same rhythm as his tongue moving within her. It was unfair. He was an experienced man, well schooled in pleasuring a woman. She was an untried girl.

Truth be told, she matched him touch for touch. Within minutes, he was trembling like a boy, on the verge of losing all control. If there was any chance to stop, it had to be now.

Slowly, he pulled away, grimacing at what felt like actual pain. She protested softly and reached out for him, but he caught her hands in one of his and shook his head.

Hoarsely, he said, "Don't. This was more than I expected ... much more. I can't be responsible ..."

She lay back against the moss, her hair a golden cloud around her head, and looked at him. No words passed between them, but there was understanding all the same. He saw it in her eyes, which seemed suddenly to hold all the world, saw the surprise and wonder, the yearning and still, thank heaven, the caution.

Her own wariness strengthened his. He would do the right thing even if it killed him, which, he thought wryly, seemed a real possibility at the moment. Every inch of his body ached. Fire raged in his blood. He had left behind his normally calm, rational mind.

Slowly, he stood and held out a hand to draw her up. "Are you all right?" he asked.

She nodded but did not speak. They walked to the horses. Nash untied the reins and helped Deanna into the seat. She averted her eyes as they passed the fallen men.

When they reached the road, Nash handed the reins to her. "You know the way. I'll keep watch."

She nodded, appearing relieved to have a task on which to concentrate. It had grown cooler. He took his frock coat off and laid it over her shoulders. She shot him a quick, grateful smile and turned back to the horses.

They traveled northward. An hour passed and then another. The track forked twice more and turned back on itself more times than Nash could count. Belatedly, he realized that without Deanna, he would never have found his way. But then he wouldn't have been alive to try.

He owed her his life. It was a strange sensation to be so beholden to another individual—especially a woman. No woman had done as much for him since his long-dead mother brought him into the world, only to promptly leave it herself. His whole life, he had looked to women for pleasure, nothing more. This was different, far beyond the limits of ordinary relationships. It was a realm he hesitated to enter. Surely once involved, he would have no greater luck traveling the labyrinthine byways than he could finding his way through this forest thicket.

The road widened. Deanna straightened her shoulders. She looked very weary but determined. Softly, she urged the horses on. For the first time in a long while, she spoke. "It isn't much farther."

He nodded and shifted the musket in his hand. He had kept it there, primed and ready, since leaving the shelter of the trees. But the renegades were long gone. Only the solitary flight of an owl and some scurrying in the trees disturbed the night silence.

They rounded a bend in the road. Ahead lay the dark silhouette of a house, the first they had seen for many miles. "Uncle Duncan's," Deanna said as she drew rein.

No light shone in the house. It appeared that all within were asleep. But barely had the wagon rolled to a stop than a shuttered window was opened on the ground floor and a man peered out.

The barrel of a musket preceded him. He was taking no chances. "Who's there?"

"Friends," Nash called out. "The one you were told to expect and another."

"It's me, Deanna. I came to show him the way."

The shutters were flung aside. A moment later, the front door of the farmhouse was thrust open. The man who stood there was almost as tall as Nash but several decades older, a burly, bearded man with an unrelenting stance. When he stepped into the moonlight, his face was incredulous.

"Deanna? Is it really you?"

She slid from the seat and went to him. "It is, Uncle Duncan. I hope you don't mind."

The man lowered his musket. "Mind? Sweet lord, girl, you're as welcome a sight as I've ever seen. But how do you come to be here?" He looked from her to Nash and back again. Some ripple in the air between them made him frown. "I don't understand."

"I was wounded and sought shelter in Mistress Marlowe's stable," Nash said. He stepped from the wagon but made no move to join Deanna. Whatever differences there were between the Marlowe brothers, they clearly did not extend to the honor of their womenfolk. "She was kind enough to help me."

"So I see," Duncan said as he loomed over her protectively. His manner gentled somewhat as he faced Deanna. "I suppose I don't have to tell you how foolish this was?"

"What should I have done?" she asked quietly. "The British were looking for him. If I'd left him where he was, or worse yet, let him go off on his own, they would have found him for sure."

"True," Duncan acknowledged. He shook his head. "Still, it's a hell of a mess. If your father finds out, he'll have my hide, and Nash's, too."

"Then I suggest we don't tell him. Now if you don't mind, I could do with a bit of rest." Without looking at either man, she stepped briskly into the house.

Duncan and Nash eyed each other. The older man relented first. Sighing, he said, "Women. Be a dull world without them."

"Indisputably. Still, she is a complication."

Duncan laughed, a short bark that was both affectionate and rueful. "She's that, all right. Always was. I meant it, though. If her father gets wind—"

"As she said, it would be best if he didn't." Nash glanced up at the moon flirting behind the leafy branches of the trees. "We have a few hours left until dawn. Let us see to our business."

Duncan nodded curtly. He stood aside to let Nash enter the house. The front room was empty. Soft footsteps sounded above.

"My daughter's room is above. She married half a year ago and moved away. Deanna will sleep there."

Nash took his eyes from the ceiling and nodded. Would she sleep after the events in the forest? And if she did, what would she dream of, death staining the trampled earth or life soaring above the trees?

He would not know. In hours, he would be done and gone. Grimly, he moved to a nearby table and withdrew the map folded in his pocket. Duncan brought a lantern. Together, the two men bent over the paper. Their talk was low and urgent, and went on for some time.

Chapter Nine

Lucas lowered the hoe he had been using to weed the kitchen garden and put his hand up to shade his eyes. There was dust on the road. Someone coming.

"Martha."

The older woman stuck her head out the back door. She squinted in the same direction he was looking. "Please, Lord," she murmured.

They hurried out past the stone wall and the gate to stand together, watching. The dust came closer. The rattle of a wagon and the familiar snort of horses rose above the lazy drone of insects.

Deanna was sitting on the seat, the reins in her hands. Beside her was a strapping young man, blond haired and broad shouldered, with a musket balanced on a knee. A second man, almost twin to the first, rode in the back.

"There you are!" Martha exclaimed. She tried hard to look stern but failed, so great was her relief. "We were worried sick. What were you thinking of, going off like that?"

"Hush, now," Lucas murmured. More that Martha, he had seen the utter weariness stamped on Deanna's finely drawn features. Gently, he laid a hand on the older woman's arm. "Be time for that later."

Martha relented, but as soon as Deanna got out of the wagon she quickly stepped forward and hugged the young woman fiercely. "Are you all right?" she asked, her voice quavering.

Deanna managed a tired smile. "I'm fine." She gestured to the two young men. "You remember Sean and Colin?"

"This can't be them," Martha protested. "They were little sprouts last time I saw them."

Lucas laughed all the harder when Duncan's sons flushed. In the five years since war had driven a wedge through the family, they had grown from gangly boys to strong men. So far, Duncan had managed to keep them from the fighting. But he didn't kid himself. Unless the war ended soon, he stood to lose them both.

"We just came along in case of trouble," Colin said. He was the older of the two.

From the back of the wagon, Sean shrugged regretfully. "There wasn't any."

"Come in and have some cold cider before you start back," Deanna suggested.

Without further encouragement, they leapt down from the wagon and untied their horses. As they hitched them in front of the house, Sean said softly, "It looks just like it always did."

"We've missed this place," Colin said. He was the more outspoken of the brothers, while Sean tended to be somewhat gentler and more thoughtful. "I remember all the fun we had down on the beach when we were growing up. You remember, De?"

Deanna nodded. She looked away, not quite trusting herself. "It's been hard on all of us."

Looking at the three bright haired young people, Martha sniffed. "Come on in now," she said, and bustled ahead into the kitchen.

Lucas took the wagon to the stable. He came into the house a few minutes later after settling the horses. A frock coat was slung over his arm.

"This yours?" he asked Colin.

"No, it's—"

Deanna reached out quickly and took the coat. "Someone forgot it. I'll take care of it."

The older man's eyebrows went up but he said nothing more. Duncan's sons drank their cider. The talk was low and soft and broken by frequent stretches of silence. After a time they left, riding home through the slanting shadows of afternoon.

Lucas went back to his weeding, and Martha took her nap. Alone in her bedroom under the eaves, Deanna laid the frock coat on her bed. She smoothed the fine wool absently as she thought of the man who had placed it over her shoulders, the man for whom she had killed. The man who had awakened her to passion unlike any she had ever known.

Edward Nash was gone, vanishing into the dark before she awoke. She could not expect to ever see him again. If she had half the sense she credited herself with, she would be profoundly grateful for that. He turned her life topsy turvy and filled her with longings that were as frightening as they were exhilarating.

There was no place for jitters and day dreams in a life where survival had to be the only priority. She had to believe that in time she would forget him. But the hollow ache at the center of her being said otherwise. Lifting the frock coat, she buried her face against it. The fabric smelled of sun and grass, leather and man. It was an oddly comforting scent.

Slowly, she sank into the chair beside the window, the coat still in her lap. Tiredness swept over her. Although she had slept the previous night, it had been only for a few hours and badly. Now her eyes fluttered shut and her breathing deepened.

The sun had drifted westward behind the trees when she was awakened by sounds in the front yard. She jumped up and peered out the window. A sudden surge of pleasure rose in her. Her father was home safely. But the happiness at his return died in an instant when she realized who he had brought with him.

Charles Peter Harrow had dismounted. He stood looking around with frank interest. At six feet, hard and trim with light brown hair and aquiline features, he was every bit as handsome as Deanna remembered. His appearance should have overjoyed her. Instead, it filled her with dread.

Gold flashed at his shoulders. He turned, caught sight of her and raised a scarlet-clad arm in greeting.

Chapter Ten

"Could have knocked me over with a feather," Nathaniel said. He sat in his favorite armchair in the front parlor, his long legs stretched out in front of him, a glass of brandy in his hand and a satisfied smile on his face.

Deanna sat on the settee nearby. Charles was by the window, also sipping brandy, gazing at her fondly.

"Ran into him in Fruncis Tavern," Nathaniel went on. "Only just got off the boat. Quite a surprise."

Deanna managed a weak smile. She was still deeply shaken by Charles's sudden appearance and the contradictory feelings it set off in her. This was the man she supposedly loved and whom she might have married a few years before. By all rights, she should be overwhelmed with delight to have him there. But instead, she could think of little except how very different he was from Edward Nash.

The American spy was danger and passion, fiery promise, challenge and desire—all the things that had been missing from her staid, safe, workaday world.

Whereas Charles was...was what? She hadn't seen him in more than five years. He looked little changed, only a bit heavier and more mature.

It was she who was different, different in ways he could not see or even begin to suspect. He had known a protected, even somewhat spoiled girl who took for granted that life would always offer her happiness. But she was a woman now, in mind if not fully in body, far wiser and more aware of how treacherous life could be.

"I've been seconded to General Clinton's staff," Charles said, oblivious to her troubled thoughts. "He's assigned me to be liaison with General Tyron here in Belle Haven. Unfortunately, I'll have to travel back and forth to New York fairly often, but at least I won't be a complete stranger."

"Couldn't have worked out better, could it?" Nathaniel asked. He was as satisfied as if he had personally arranged the matter.

"I didn't realize you were in the army," Deanna said weakly. She still couldn't get used to the sight of Charles in the bold scarlet uniform, redolent as it was of arrogant confidence and the relentless will to dominate. He had seemed a gentler man, yet the uniform suited him.

"I only just bought my commission. Frankly, with Father still going strong, there wasn't a great deal for me to do at home. I thought it would be a good time to see a bit of the world, while serving King and Country, of course."

"Of course," she murmured.

"I imposed on a few friends to see that I was billeted over here." Abruptly, he blurted, "I must say, Deanna, you're a sight for sore eyes."

Nathaniel laughed as he set his brandy on the sideboard and stood up. "I like a man who's not afraid to speak his mind. How long are you staying this time, Harrow?"

"At least a week, sir. General Tyron is giving a ball and he expects all of the officers to appear. I wonder if Deanna would like to accompany me?"

"Why don't you ask her yourself? I've work to be done." With a nod at them both, Nathaniel sauntered out of the room.

Deanna stared after him in dismay. Her father had never left her alone with a male over the age of fifteen. He knew that in the ordinary course of her day, she often encountered men alone, but when he was around she was never left unchaperoned. She supposed it was his way of making a point. And it had worked. Until now. Now he had quite deliberately, even pointedly, gone off and left her alone with Charles. The message couldn't have been clearer.

Charles cleared his throat. He advanced toward the settee and slowly lowered himself upon it. Hesitantly, he took Deanna's hands in his. "I don't think I realized until now how much I missed you."

Her cheeks warmed. "That's kind of you," she murmured.

"I mean it. We only had a few months together when you were in England, but I knew then that you were the woman for me. I should have declared myself. Instead, I foolishly let you go thinking I would join you shortly and we would have a chance to get to know each other better. It was a mistake.''

Charles was not given to long speeches; this was the most talk she had ever heard from him. And she could not recall him ever expressing his feelings more clearly. Her throat tightened. This should have been the most glorious moment of her life, but instead it only filled her with dread. She had a sudden, terrible fear that he was actually about to propose. In an almost desperate bid to prevent that, she said, "This ball the general is giving, do tell me about it.''

Charles looked a bit startled at her sudden interest, but recovered manfully. "Well, as to that, I don't really know much about it, only that he's giving it, of course, and that he expects a good turnout.'' Realizing belatedly that he was making the affair sound too much like a duty call, he added, "Bound to be fun, don't you think? Show the colors and all that.''

Showing colors—British, American, any at all—was not to Deanna's taste. She had long ago decided on a stance of strict neutrality in order to stay loyal to both sides of her divided family and to carry out her duties as a healer. But she could hardly tell Charles that.

Instead, she smiled faintly. "Sounds a bit ambitious. I can't remember the last time there was a social event in these parts.''

Charles grimaced. His hands tightened on hers. "You poor little thing. I really do blame myself. I should have come and gotten you, taken you away from all this. When I think how deprived you've been—''

''Actually, we've managed quite well,'' Deanna interjected. He appeared to be working himself into a fervor, something she most certainly did not want. Briskly, she pulled her hands away from his and stood up. ''It is good to see you, Charles.'' Good didn't really describe it but she was determined to be polite.

He rose, frowning but left no choice. Courtesy constrained them both. ''Yes, well, I suppose I should be going...''

''If you must. I do have quite a few chores I need to see to.''

They walked to the door together, Deanna doing her best not to hurry.

''About the ball,'' Charles said.

''The ball, yes, of course.'' She did not want to go. The very thought filled her with dread, but there was absolutely no way she could refuse without disappointing her father and hurting Charles. Neither man deserved such treatment.

''I will be honored to go with you.'' She was rewarded by the relieved smile that wreathed his features. When their eyes met, she noticed that his were warm with approval and something more—something she would not have been able to recognize even a day before.

''Until then,'' he said and raised her hand to his lips again.

Chapter Eleven

"Hold still," Martha said through a mouthful of pins. "I swear, you wiggle more than a worm on a fishhook."

Deanna grimaced. "Maybe because that's how I feel."

Martha looked up from where she was trying to pin the hem of Deanna's dress. "Why?" she demanded. "Because you're going to a ball? How many girls do you think would like to be in your spot?"

"Plenty," Deanna admitted. "I know I sound horribly ungrateful but—"

"No buts. Charles Harrow is a fine man. Besides, you could do with a touch of fun."

Deanna bit back a sigh. There was no point arguing with the woman. Ever since she learned of Charles's arrival, Martha had been in a romantic frenzy. Charles was the answer to all her concerns. He would whisk Deanna away from her dangerous surroundings, bestow upon her the position and material well-being she fully deserved and spend the rest of his life being a loving, protective husband. In short, he was perfect, which meant that the dress had to be, too.

Deanna didn't want to ask where Martha had gotten the flowered muslin for the bodice and overskirt or the rose silk for the petticoat, much less the delicate Flanders lace to trim the wrists and neckline of what promised to be the loveliest gown she had ever possessed. Such luxuries had long since vanished from the war-torn country. Sea captains who managed to run the British blockades brought in far more important goods, namely weapons. Only very rarely did anything else slip by.

But Martha had her ways—and her friends. She was rightly pleased with herself, and Deanna didn't have the heart to change that. She took as deep a breath as she could manage and made a valiant effort not to move.

Directly opposite Deanna was a full-size mirror set in a mahogany standing frame. The mirror was very old. It had belonged to Amelia Daniels Marlowe. The glass needed to be resilvered but it was still clear enough for Deanna to be startled by the sight of the woman reflected in it.

It had been so long since she had seen herself in anything other than plain, serviceable clothes that she had forgotten what she could look like in anything different. The woman in the mirror was a stranger, a creature of cool beauty and elegance who eyed her levelly, revealing nothing of her thoughts.

Sweet heaven, was that her? More to the point, was that how she would look to Charles? Innocent she might still be, unaware she was not. Martha's comment about the worm had been more fitting than she had realized, for surely the woman in the mirror was intended to bait a baronet. She cleared her throat and ventured a tentative suggestion. "The neckline is a bit low, don't you think?"

Martha didn't even deign to look up. "You're not a wee lass any more, are you?"

"I'm not a married woman, either." And she didn't intend to become one any time soon. "It's not appropriate for me—"

Martha muttered something under her breath and stood up laboriously. She made a show of massaging her knees as though to emphasize that she was an old, weak woman deserving of better treatment. But there was nothing weak in her manner as she demanded, "Deanna Marlowe, what is the matter with you? I've never seen you like this." More gently, she added, "Child, whatever troubles you, tell me. I'm not so old that I don't remember what it's like between a maid and a man. There can be many a rough spot along the road before a soft bed is reached."

"It's not like that—" Deanna began, only to break off when she realized that it was exactly like that. The problem was that the man vying for her attention was Charles Harrow. Not Edward Nash.

Heaven help her, she was still thinking about the American. Her face flamed. She averted her eyes from the mirror and said softly, "There's nothing wrong, Martha, truly."

It was the greatest lie she had ever told, and she feared her bright cheeks would give her away. But the older woman, though she appeared far from convinced, gave quarter. She went back to her pinning and shortly had it done.

"There," Martha said, satisfied. "Take it off careful now."

Deanna complied. She put her homespun dress back on with relief. The gown lay spread out on her bed like a hothouse flower sprouting at the edge of a barren field. "It is beautiful," she said, unable to hide her longing. If only the world were different, if only she were the young, carefree girl she had been.

"And so will you be," Martha said. She patted Deanna's cheek with her careworn hand, gathered up the gown and was gone.

Deanna stood at the window, staring out at the verdant landscape. She had been penned up all morning and could bear it no longer. On the spur of the moment, she tugged on her oldest leather boots, grabbed her bonnet and hurried down the stairs.

Nathaniel had gone into town. Lucas was about his chores. Martha sat in the kitchen, the gown in her lap, humming softly to herself as she stitched. She seemed sublimely happy, undoubtedly imagining what the ball would be like.

Deanna felt guilty as she sneaked past her and slipped out the front door. She should be able to share Martha's enthusiasm but all she could muster was a dull sort of apprehension.

The day demanded better. Sparkling sunlight, air scented by the sea and the cacophony of birdsong beckoned her away from unhappy thoughts. Deanna didn't hesitate. She headed straight toward the beach.

Guilty pleasure bore her along. She walked, swinging her bonnet, which she truly had meant to put on, until she came to the sand. There she paused beneath a twining blackberry bush to remove her boots, leaving them along with her bonnet.

The sand was warm and ticklish between her toes. Picking up her skirts, she ran lightly to the water's edge. Foam flecked wavelets played catch along the length of the beach. Sandpipers darted out as a flock of brown pelicans bobbed fifty feet from shore. Deanna laughed with the sheer joy of it all. After the confusion and worry of the past few days, she felt reborn. She pulled the ribbon from her hair and let it flow behind her on the wind as she ran down the beach.

For a moment, she was tempted to do as she had as a child, find a secluded spot, shuck her clothes and go swimming. But she was a child no longer, and the fact remained that many boats frequented the waters around Belle Haven. Privacy could be a fleeting thing.

Instead, she compromised by hoisting up her skirts to mid-thigh and wading into the water. Small fish darted around her legs, and crabs skittered out of the way. Lobsters moved lazily among clumps of seaweed. Farther up the beach, black mussels gleamed on the rocks where the tide had lately covered them.

Deanna couldn't resist. She remembered too well the seafood stews of her childhood and how they had always tasted best when she did the catching herself. Bending slightly so that her long hair trailed in the water, she plucked a lobster from its watery den, taking due care not to be clawed, and dropped it into her upheld skirt. Several crabs followed. She moved up the sand to the rocks, collecting mussels as she went.

So intent was she that she did not notice the man standing half concealed in the shadows of the nearby pine trees, watching her.

Chapter Twelve

Nash grimaced at the taut hardness of his manhood. He was a fool to have come here, a fool to ask for more trouble than he'd already had. A fool to be longing after a woman who should mean nothing to him.

Angrily, he turned away from the sight on the beach. He had not expected to find her like this. It had never occurred to him that she would be any place but at home, tending her chores with her servants nearby, and possibly also her father, who was known to have returned. It was the challenge as much as anything else that had driven him to take such a feckless risk.

He had thought—if he thought about it at all—to surprise her, claim the return of his frock coat as his excuse and conduct a few minutes of chaste conversation during which he would thank her politely for saving his life twice and then formally take his leave.

All so much fluff, he thought, disgruntled. He had really wanted to reassure himself that the sudden appearance of one Charles Peter Harrow, *baronet,* had not changed her. But of course it must have. She was only human, after all, a woman as susceptible as any to the blandishments of wealthy, powerful men.

Truth be told, he had used those self-same blandishments to good effect himself. He could hardly blame that Harrow chap for doing the same, damn him to hell for all eternity.

His hands clenched. This had to stop. He had a mission, people were depending on him. Never had he shirked his duty, no matter how painful or difficult. No reason to start now at this most critical of turning points.

Silently, he moved away from the beach but the image of the golden woman laughing with a child's pleasure among the caressing waves stayed with him. He could not get it from his mind. That most likely explained his distraction, and how it came to be that he, experienced woodsman and ardent practitioner of stealth, was taken by surprise.

The man dropped ten feet ahead of him, coming out of the trees to land upright on the path, blocking Nash's way. He was tall and rangy, dressed in deerskins, with a musket slung over his back, a knife in his hand and a hood pulled down to conceal his features.

Edward crouched, cursing under his breath, and in an instant had his own knife out. Behind him a soft thud announced that the other man was not alone. Nash could not afford to turn around to see who else was there. Instead, he moved forward cautiously, trying to maneuver into a better position. The man blocked him at every turn. There seemed to be no alternative to a fight that would, at the least, be bloody. But suddenly, the man straightened, put his hands on his hips and laughed.

"I don't believe it," he said as he pulled the hood off. "Edward Nash ambushed. There's one for the record books."

Nash scowled even as he sheathed his knife. He was embarrassed and determined not to show it. "Haven't you anything better to do, Wesskum, besides run around in the woods playing children's games?"

"Game, is it? You wouldn't have thought it was funny if I'd been a Brit."

"If you'd been a Brit," Nash said succinctly, "you'd be dead." He nodded his head toward the second man. "You and your friend here."

Wesskum grinned. "Big talker." He nodded to his companion who, after a quick glance at Nash, vanished silently into the forest. "I heard you were in these parts," Wesskum said.

The menace of a few moments before was gone. In its place was matter-of-fact pleasantness as though there was nothing out of the ordinary about them meeting in such a way. But then, Nash thought, in these times there probably wasn't. "Is there anyone who hasn't heard?" he asked, grumbling. "Maybe we ought to print up handbills. Wouldn't do to have the Brits miss anything."

"You're in a mood. What's the problem?"

"Nothing, everything's fine. I've just about got what I came for and I'll be on my way."

"Not so fast. Something's come up."

Nash's eyes narrowed. He knew Fletcher Wesskum more by reputation than anything else, although the two men had worked together occasionally in the past few years. The woodsman and scout was an ally the Americans were glad to have.

He had been born in Belle Haven of partly Indian stock that dated back generations. Although he said little about himself, and was known to disappear for weeks on end, he had a way of turning up with useful information just when it was needed most. Now, for instance.

"Did you know Tyron's giving a ball?" Wesskum asked.

Nash frowned. He had a sudden, piercing image of Deanna in Harrow's arms, dancing. "I heard."

"Did you also hear that Clinton's coming up for it with some of his officers? He and Tyron are going to use the occasion to have a face-to-face meeting."

Nash looked hard at the scout. "Are you sure of this?"

"Dead-on. Wouldn't mind being a little bug on the wall. How about you?"

"Can't say I wouldn't," Nash said thoughtfully. "If there's any way..."

Fletcher plucked a blade of grass and stuck it between his teeth. With studied casualness, he said, "There's a closet in the room where they'll meet. If somebody got in there ahead of time and managed to go undetected, who knows what might be gathered?"

"It's worth a try. Who did you have in mind?"

"I'd go myself, but unfortunately there's only one way into the room—right smack through the rest of Tyron's headquarters. I can slip through any forest on earth without being seen, as I believe you just witnessed. But the minute I set foot indoors, I stick out a mile."

He cast a daunting look at Nash. "We wouldn't happen to know somebody who can pass for a nob, would we?"

"Who're you calling a nob?"

"You, laddie. You can swag with the best of them. What do you say?"

"Might be worth a try," Nash said. He fell silent, thinking. After a time he smiled.

Chapter Thirteen

Torches lit the way to Tyron's headquarters. Up and down the road in front of the single-story wooden building, carriages and horses jostled for room. Deanna had seen nothing like it since the years before the war. She stared dumbfounded at the crush of people and animals, the darting firelight, the laughter and the music. It seemed like another world, one very far removed from her own.

Charles smiled reassuringly and patted her hand. "Have I told you how lovely you look?"

She sat back against the padded leather seat of the carriage. "Several times."

Aside from a slight flush he was unrepentant. "It bears repeating. You were beautiful enough in London five years ago, but now..." A certain light came into his eyes. He leaned closer.

Hastily, she said, "I believe the line is moving."

He withdrew reluctantly, and a few minutes later they were able to leave the carriage with a stable hand in front of General Tyron's headquarters, which was situated a short distance from the river landing. In peacetime, the building had been a tavern where barges and other vessels customarily put in. Just down the broad, hard-packed road was a popular stable and across from it was the church. In front of the church was the town green, which legend had it Amelia Daniels had laid out.

In its earliest years, the church had been the site of a meetinghouse and fort where the first inhabitants of Belle Haven had been forced to take shelter during an attack by renegade Pequots. Not until several decades later did they feel safe enough to remove the high, protective walls and add a church onto the meetinghouse.

Even in the midst of war—or perhaps especially then—the church was a busy place on a Sunday morning. But at the moment, the former tavern was the focus of all attention.

On Charles's arm, Deanna climbed the three narrow steps to the wooden porch. The double doors stood open. She caught sight of scarlet-clad men and gaily gowned women milling about inside.

Apart from the women, very few civilians were in evidence, and those, well-known Tory supporters. With the exception of her father, who had passed the event off as being "for the young people," it looked as though most everyone had accepted General Tyron's invitation.

Charles signalled a passing servant and got them both a drink—Rhenish wine for himself, cider for her. She took a sip while eyeing the room over the rim of her glass. General Tyron was holding court in a corner of the main room, surrounded by a group of officers. He was a short, round-faced man of stocky build with a pugnacious expression and somewhat florid features.

Deanna disliked him intensely for the brutal way he treated Belle Haven's inhabitants, but she knew better than to let her feelings show. As Charles drew her over to be introduced, she settled her features into what she hoped was an amicable expression and took a firm grip on her temper.

Tyron saw them coming. He broke off his conversation with a young, eager-to-please lieutenant and smiled benignly. "How nice to see you, Miss Marlowe. Your father mentioned you'd be coming by." Turning his attention to Charles, he added, "Do I gather I'll be seeing you often in Belle Haven, Major?"

The young officers relegated to the background eyed Charles with envy and admiration as he responded. "Yes, sir, you've gathered correctly."

Tyron laughed. He was said to like people who weren't afraid of him, perhaps because there were so few of them. "Good lad. Clinton speaks well of you. I hope he's right. We're riding into difficult times."

It was on the tip of Deanna's tongue to point out that they had been in them for quite a while now. The British hadn't even considered the possibility of the war dragging on five years. They had expected a quick, decisive victory, and indeed, in the early months of the conflict, it had seemed they would get it. But the Americans had rallied and against all expectations had managed to hold on. It was whispered now that they had even gained the advantage. Unless the British could end the struggle soon they might actually lose.

Defiantly, a tremor of pleasure ran through her at the thought. With her precious neutrality more at risk than ever before, she was glad of a sudden disruption by the door that diverted Tyron's attention.

He swept forward to greet the man who had just arrived. Loudly, so that all could hear, he said, "General Clinton, welcome. I trust you and your men are well rested from your journey and prepared for our revels?"

The tall, genteel man he addressed frowned slightly. Unlike Tyron, Clinton had a reputation for restraint. He prided himself on being a gentleman and never allowed the war to get in the way of proper conduct.

"Rested, yes," he said. "As for the revels, I trust they will be properly restrained as is keeping with the times."

Tyron's brows knit. Clearly, restraint was not his chief concern. But Clinton was the senior officer, and Tyron was far too adept to oppose him directly. Instead, he merely shrugged. "Of course. But the good people of Belle Haven—loyalists all—will be disappointed if we turn aside their hospitality."

Having thus neatly transformed the ball into a testament of support for King and Country they could not possibly discourage, he led Clinton forward to the groaning board and signaled a servant to make sure everyone had a drink.

"A toast," Tyron said when they had all been served. "To His Most August Majesty, King George III."

Voices rang out, "Hear, hear." Glasses were solemnly lifted. A hearty baritone began to sing "God Save the King," with the others quickly joining in.

Or most of the others. Deanna stood mute. If necessary, she would claim later that she had a poor singing voice and did not wish to disgrace herself. Several of the other women, she noticed, appeared to have the same affliction. As for the men, they were oblivious, caught up as they were in the ringing proclamation of their allegiance.

At length, the song was done and conversation resumed. Charles introduced Deanna to several of his fellow officers, all up from New York with Clinton. They were faultlessly cordial even if their eyes did tend to linger rather longer—and lower—than she would have liked.

She blamed the dress, which fit her to perfection. Martha had outdone herself. No woman in the room was better gowned, not even those who through their husbands—or lovers—had access to smuggled goods.

Certainly, Charles approved of her appearance. He barely took his eyes off her as they circulated around the room. Deanna found the exercise boring until it dawned on her that he was showing her off with a proprietary air that the other men could not possibly miss. Resigned to making the best of it, she was relieved when he suggested that they dance. An impromptu ballroom had been set up outside with planks of wood laid over the ground and lit torches lashed to posts.

"It's hardly London," Charles said as he led her out, "but it will make for an amusing story years from now, how we danced under the moon in the midst of war."

Deanna's throat tightened. He was presuming a great deal, yet in all honesty she had done nothing to discourage him. Her coolness was no more than was proper for a well-bred young woman. As for her thoughts, they were entirely her own, unconfided to anyone.

The dance was a minuet, for which she was thankful. Its intricate steps demanded concentration and separated her from Charles at regular intervals.

They were back together for the pirouette when her glance happened to turn in the direction of the doors leading into the building. For a moment, she froze and only with difficulty managed to resume the steps.

The dance ended. Deanna looked frantically around, telling herself she could not possibly have seen what she thought she had. She had just begun to shrug off her folly when Charles suddenly raised a hand in gesture.

In a pleased voice, he called, "Nash!"

Chapter Fourteen

Hearing his name, Edward stopped just as he was about to enter the building. He spotted the man bearing down on him. With a muttered curse on his lips, he strode forward to greet Charles.

"Harrow, I heard you were around. What sort of fancy maneuvering got you this billet?"

"Pure enterprise, my boy, nothing less. It's been a dog's age since I've seen you. How have you been?"

"Middling. Yourself?"

"Can't complain. I heard you were back this way. Any particular reason?"

Nash shrugged. He had scrupulously avoided looking at Deanna but knew that he couldn't keep that up much longer. For one thing, it would look too suspicious. For another, his self control simply didn't stretch that far. "It seemed a decent enough place to be," he said. "I don't believe I've had the pleasure, Miss...?"

"Miss Deanna Marlowe," Charles said. He put his arm around Deanna's waist in an unmistakably possessive gesture. "We're old friends. In fact, I requested this posting so that I could call on Miss Marlowe again."

Nash bared his teeth in a feral smile. "How comforting to know that the war isn't inconveniencing you, Charles. Are you from around here, Miss Marlowe?"

Her eyes flashed dangerously. For a moment, he thought she was going to tell him off. But she got a grip on herself and merely scowled. "I was born in Belle Haven, Mr.?"

"Nash," Charles said quickly. "Edward Nash. We were at school together."

Deanna's eyes widened. "In England?"

Charles laughed. "Of course in England. Where did you think?"

"I didn't... That is, Mr. Nash sounds rather American."

Charles groaned in mock dismay. "Now you've done it. I assure you, Edward, she doesn't usually insult people she's just met."

Deanna opened her mouth again, undoubtedly to say something improper, but Nash forestalled her. Smoothly, he said, "No insult taken. Miss Marlowe can't be expected to know about my... shall we say mixed background."

He turned to Deanna and with a kindly air continued. "My mother was from Virginia originally. My father was British. I was born here but educated there, and I like to think that I'm at home on either side."

"I'll just bet you do," Deanna muttered.

Startled, Charles looked at her. "What was that?"

"Nothing," she said quickly. She took Charles's arm and stared at him through the thick fringe of her lashes with a display of coquettishness that made Nash frown. Ignoring him, she said, "The music is starting again and you're such a wonderful dancer it would be a shame to miss an opportunity."

Harrow appeared surprised by her sudden flirtatiousness but more than willing to give in to it. Nash was about to turn away in disgust at the wiles of shameless females when they were suddenly interrupted.

A young aide to Clinton appeared at Charles's side. "Excuse me, Major, the general would like to have a word with you."

Reluctant though he was, Charles could not ignore the call to duty. Yet neither did he want to disappoint Deanna. Under the circumstances, what could be more natural than to turn to a convenient friend? "Would you mind, Nash? It's not fair to Deanna to have to sit out, and you're not a bad dancer yourself."

"Oh, no," Deanna said quickly, "that's quite all right. I wouldn't want to impose on—"

"It's no imposition," Nash assured her, a mocking light in his eyes as he sketched a quick bow. "What are friends for?"

"Good man," Charles said. He placed Deanna's hand in Edward's, awarded them both a benign smile and followed the young officer.

Barely had he gone than Deanna snatched her hand back and glared at Nash. "Please don't trouble yourself. Charles means well, but if he had any notion about you—"

"Actually, he knows me quite well. We were at school together, after all."

She paled. Keeping her voice very low, she said, "I can't tell if you're mocking me or him, but I do know I want no part of it. Good evening."

Without hesitation, his hand lashed out. Bronzed fingers closed around her wrist. She resisted. He refused to let her go.

Thus they stood, unnoticed in the milling crowd but in danger of drawing attention at any moment. Still, neither was willing to give in. Just as the standoff seemed certain to continue dangerously long, Deanna relented.

"All right, I'll dance with you. But that's an end to it. After that, I don't want to see you again."

"Fine," Nash muttered. He let go of her wrist, put her arm through his and led her onto the dance floor, just in time for the strains of the ländler to begin.

The dance was of German origin, made popular in Britain by the Hanoverian kings and thought by some to be scandalous because it involved men and women touching far more than was usual. Nash had always liked it, but now he cursed his bad luck. The last thing he wanted to do was hold Deanna Marlowe in his arms.

Gingerly, he drew her to him. "Relax, it'll be over soon."

"Not soon enough," she said and made a point of not looking at him as the dance began.

And yet, neither was immune to the music and the night, the torches leaping high and, more importantly, the nagging sense of war. By degrees, hesitantly and with real resistance, anger fled. Suspicion subsided. Other feelings, no less fierce but entirely different in their nature, reawakened.

She was as a wand in his hands, slender and pliant but with undeniable strength. Her perfume filled his breath. The silken smoothness of her skin dazzled as precious jewels could not. He felt surrounded by feminity in its purest, most essential form, without the frippery of falsehood, proud and challenging, calling to him in an ancient way he could not deny.

He remembered the touch of her hands on him when he lay bleeding and in pain. The look in her eyes after she fired the musket that brought down the renegade. The weary courage with which she had refused to abandon him, insisting instead on seeing him to safey. The playful, innocent joy with which she teased the ocean waves, oblivious to his presence. And the ability to make him rigid with desire with a flick of a glance from the corner of her eye, a toss of her head, a mere breath of sound.

Madness enveloped them under the moon as they danced in the circle of torchlight. Absolute, unalloyed madness.

And yet, Nash could not for the life of him deny what she released in him—the need to possess and protect, the longing to trust, the conviction that here at last, however unlikely, was a woman he would forget not, even into eternity.

A foolishly romantic notion, to be sure, the kind that got men killed. But one he could not shake no matter how desperately he tried. Although with her in his arms he was perhaps not struggling quite as valiantly as he might.

Or struggling at all, for when he did at last speak to her, the words seemed to come from a man who was ready to admit defeat. "I need your help," he said.

Chapter Fifteen

Surely she had heard wrong? He couldn't possibly have said what Deanna thought he had. "My help?"

Nash nodded. In a low, urgent voice, he said, "I'm going to disappear in a few minutes. If anyone asks where I am, it would help greatly if you'd say I wasn't feeling well and went off to get some fresh air."

"Not well? air?"

"I realize this is unusual, but—"

"Unusual? It's bizarre. What are you talking about?"

"Lower your voice. If anyone overhears you, it's my hide on the line, not yours."

If he thought she could be so easily bowled over, he was very much mistaken. Never mind how devastatingly handsome he looked in black velvet breeches and a black frock coat with a splash of white lace at his chest and cuffs. Never mind the bronzed skin stretched taut over finely chiseled bone and sinew, the sweep of ebony hair in a queue at the back of his neck, the aura of male strength and will that hung about him.

The sudden acceleration of her pulse coursed through her. "You cannot possibly expect me to be such a fool. I have no idea what game you're playing but I will tell you this, if you bring harm to Uncle Duncan, I swear before God that I'll hunt you down like the swine you are and finish you myself."

It should have been a ludicrous threat but Nash didn't laugh. He appeared to take it seriously. "Your uncle's perfectly safe. Just because I was schooled in England and know Harrow doesn't make me one of them."

"How do I know that? It's possible that you're working both sides. Why should I trust you?"

His mouth tightened. He could feel his anger mounting and wondered if it would break free. But instead, he took a visible grip on himself and said, "Because you saved my life. If you believe the Chinese, as I do, that makes you responsible for it."

"Of all the outrageous—"

"Temper. I'm not asking you for the world, only to cover for me if it should become necessary."

"Cover what? You could be doing absolutely anything. You can't possibly expect me to—"

Color darkened his high-boned cheeks. With a muttered curse, he swept her off toward the edge of the dance floor where they were less likely to be observed. "You are a most infuriating woman."

Deanna ignored the rapid beating of her heart and feigned a sweet smile. "Thank you."

"I mean it. No wonder you're attracted to Harrow. You know you can twist him around your little finger. Well, there happen to be men made of sterner stuff."

Daring greatly, she tilted her head and met his eyes. The light in them jolted her. Truly, this was no patient, courtly Charles Harrow. This was a man she would do very well not to toy with.

Knowing that was not enough. Boldly, with the air of one stepping out into thin air, she said, "If you think you're one of them, you should need no help from me. Nor will you get any unless I'm convinced it's merited."

"You weren't so stingy last time."

She flushed, thinking exactly of the liberties she had permitted. "All the same, I will not be kept in ignorance."

"Not even when knowing may endanger you?"

"Danger lies in ignorance," she countered.

"Has anyone suggested to you that women are supposed to be demure and compliant?"

"Yes, but I didn't take it seriously."

He sighed and looked heavenward as though in search of divine inspiration. Finding none, he shook his head in resignation. "All right, but not here."

"Where?"

By way of answer, he drew her farther away from the dance floor, into the shadows beyond the flickering torches. There, in the hushed stillness of the night, Deanna struggled to regain her breath. The boldness in the midst of the crowd was gone. She was suddenly, vividly aware of being alone with him.

"We should go back," she began.

"We will, in a moment. But first—" He moved slightly so that her back was to a stalwart oak and he was standing very close. His head bent, shading her from the light of the moon. "You wanted truth."

"An explanation, a reason . . ."

"Truth."

His breath was warm, lightly scented with brandy, arousing to a degree she never would have believed possible if she hadn't already experienced this feeling with him once before.

And all that merely with a kiss. For an instant, she allowed herself to imagine what it would be like if more had happened between them. The thought alone was enough to make her hastily back away. But the oak was against her, Nash was before her, and the night was suddenly spinning out of control.

"No," she said and put a hand to his chest, holding him off.

He stopped.

The corners of his mouth twitched. "Why, Mistress Marlowe, what is it you imagine I'm about to do?"

Embarrassment shot through her. "You . . . I . . ."

"Yes?" he drawled. "Was there something you wanted?"

She gave his chest another shove. Her hand touched stone lightly covered by skin and velvet. She could no more move him than she could rearrange a mountain.

He made a show of yielding and spread his hands as though in surrender. Deanna shook her head in exasperation. "Truth," she said succinctly. "The truth about you and what you are doing here. And—" she added for good measure "—I suggest you manage to tell it soon, before some of Charles's fellow officers start wondering where his good friend has taken me."

"About Charles, what exactly are your intentions toward him?"

"My intentions? Don't you mean—"

"Yours. His are clear enough."

"I fail to see why I should discuss this with you."

"His pride's his downfall."

"What is that supposed to mean?" Deanna demanded.

"Only that he was bred to arrogance. They all are. In the end it will finish them."

"They being the British?"

"Who else? They're raised to believe they're superior to everyone else. If they didn't think that, they'd have won this war a long time ago. It's only because they've consistently underestimated us that we've been able to hang on."

"Interesting theory, but this is hardly the time to examine it. Once and for all, what are you doing here?"

He sighed as though resigned to the stubbornness of women, and propped himself comfortably against the tree. Arms crossed over his chest, a pleasant smile pulling at his lips, he looked for all the world like a man taking a relaxing stroll in the woods. "I'm preparing to sneak into a closet where, if I manage not to get caught, I should be able to overhear a meeting between Clinton and Tyron. The information gleaned from it may prove vital. All I want you to do is prevent anyone from wondering where I've gone. That's not too much to ask, is it?''

She stared at him for a long moment. Nothing in his expression suggested he was telling other than the truth.

''You're mad,'' she said.

''Quite possibly, but you'll still help, won't you?''

Deanna's fists clenched. She fought against the desperate impulse to pummel some sense into him. ''Don't you realize how dangerous this is? If you make a sound or if someone just happens to look in the closet, you'll be finished. They'll drag you out of there and hang you, probably without even a trial.''

Her voice was shaking. To her horror, she felt tears burning her eyes. Frantically, she turned away, but not before Nash saw.

With a muttered exclamation, he drew her against the hard wall of his chest.

Chapter Sixteen

"Little fool," Nash said gruffly. His big hand stroked her hair with clumsy tenderness.

Deanna sniffed and rested her head against him. She really shouldn't be doing this, but it felt so good, so right. Surely just a moment or two wouldn't hurt? She couldn't remember when she had felt so safe and protected which was absurd, really, all things considered. Yet there she was, unable to quell the wayward thoughts tumbling through her.

She could feel the beat of his heart under her cheek. His strength was gentled. She raised her head and met his eyes. "I really don't want them to hang you."

He smiled a little crookedly. "So I gathered."

"Yes, well, so long as that's clear—"

He lifted a finger to catch the glittering tear slipping down her cheek. Deep in his throat, he murmured, "Don't cry."

"I'm not."

"Yes, you are." His head bent. Gently, with perfect naturalness, he caught the next tear on his lips.

A moment later, his arms wrapped taut around her and the steely hardness of his body blocked out the world. Then she tasted his lips, salty against hers. Salt and tears, sweetness and promise, all mingled together for a timeless instant.

Her lips parted, expecting the slow thrust of his tongue. They clung together, heedless of danger, until the sudden snap of a branch not far away forced them to part.

Nash let her go and took a step back, but his hand remained on her waist, steadying her. "I've changed my mind," he said, his voice rasping like water over stone. "Don't say anything. Keep out of it."

Her eyes widened, reflecting in their forest green depths a world of captured light. "Why?"

"It's too dangerous. I was wrong to involve you." He turned away and looked toward the building, his features hard. "I'll go first, you follow. We shouldn't be seen together again."

Deanna straightened. The hazy cloak of passion evaporated. She shot him a flinty eyed stare that would have felled a lesser man. "Absolutely not."

He shook his head in exasperation. "Not two minutes ago, you wanted nothing to do with it."

"I never said that."

He stared at her in disbelief. "Of course you did. It was unmistakable. You said—"

"I said you couldn't expect me to cover for you when I had no real idea of what you were doing. However, your explanation is acceptable."

"It is?"

She nodded. "Not sensible or even particularly intelligent. But I do believe you intend to spy on Clinton and Tyron. That part is clear enough."

Nash scowled. "What do you mean, not sensible or intelligent? What's wrong with it?"

"Besides the likelihood of your being hanged?"

"Don't start on that again."

"How do you know they're going to say anything useful? It seems more likely they'll just sit around, hoist a few and swap old war stories."

Her candor disconcerted him but he made a valiant effort to take it in stride. "You have a most unflattering view of the hapless male, Miss Marlowe. There are times when we do more than drink and brag."

"Certainly there are. Unfortunately, the results are usually regrettable. You could be risking your life for nothing."

For a moment, he was tempted to tell her that he had direct information about the purpose of the meeting. But that would have been unjust to Fletcher Wesskum, even without mentioning his name. "Possibly," he said.

"But you still intend to go through with it?"

Nash shrugged. "I really don't have much choice. Even the chance of getting information on their plans can't be passed up."

Deanna paled. Solemnly, she nodded. "All right then, I will help you. If anyone appears to be noticing your absence, I will say you drank too much and had to relieve yourself."

Nash winced. "Couldn't you be a bit more discreet?"

She looked puzzled. "And leave the possibility that I might not allay suspicion?"

"It would be enough to simply say I was indisposed and needed fresh air."

"I fail to see why."

"Because proper young ladies are not supposed to know about men drinking to excess or the physical results."

She sighed. "We're back to proper again?"

"No, but I do feel compelled to keep trying. Why didn't your father leave you in school in England?"

"He tried. I ran away."

"Good God, really?"

"I'm afraid so." She shrugged and looked away, unwilling to meet his eyes. "It's difficult to explain, but I love this place quite inordinately. There are times when I feel as though I could never belong anywhere else."

"Then why are you involved with Harrow?"

"I'm not," she protested.

"He thinks you are. He thinks he's going to marry you and take you back to England to serve tea, eat crumpets, ride to hounds and breed more little Harrows. I don't believe it's occurred to him for a moment that you have any significant attachment to Belle Haven. In fact," he went on remorselessly, "if anyone ever did suggest that to him, he'd think it was ludicrous."

"Why?" Deanna demanded. "There is no lovelier place on earth, and when you consider what people—including my ancestors—went through to create Belle Haven, you can hardly disregard it."

"I don't," he corrected. "But Harrow does. It's just another wide spot on the road to him. Worse yet, it's in a rebellious country populated by traitors in need of a good thrashing. He undoubtedly believes he is doing you the greatest favor by taking you away from all this."

Deanna's eyes flashed but she refused to give in to the anger he sparked. "I don't want to talk about Harrow. He's not the problem. You are. If you're really going to go ahead with this harebrained plan, then I am going to help."

He took a deep breath, visibly fighting for calm, and glared at her. "Has it occurred to you that you could come under suspicion yourself?"

She looked at him as though he had been dropped on his head a time too often. "Do you imagine I haven't already?"

"What do you mean?" A sudden thought went through him. She had a quick, astounding glimpse of Edward Nash actually looking afraid before the mask slammed down again. "No one knows you helped me, correct?"

"Only Uncle Duncan and the boys, and I don't think you need to worry about them. What I meant was that I've always made some people think twice. I got used to it a long time ago..."

Why? You're a beautiful young woman, the daughter of a wealthy and influential Tory. Why should anyone look at you askance?''

The innocence of men astounded her sometimes. They believed themselves so worldly, when often they nissed what went on right in front of them.

''I'm a healer,'' she said quietly, ''and a woman. It hasn't been   long since people like me were burned.''

He flinched and stared at her in disbelief. ''You can't be serious.''

''Oh, I know, this is supposed to be the age of reason. But people don't give up their fears that easily. The more irrational those fears are, the more inclined they are to cling to them.'' She grimaced, real pain following hard on the thought. ''There are some nights when I think I can still smell the burning lingering in the air. The trick is learning to ignore it and go on.''

Having said all she intended to on the subject, Deanna straightened her shoulders, smoothed her skirts and stepped in front of Nash. With her back to him, she touched a finger to her lips surreptitiously.

Her lips felt slightly swollen and tender. Anyone who really stopped to notice might wonder why. For all her proud speech, she understood full well the danger she was about to step into. Yet she held her head high and her shoulders straight as she walked into the torchlight.

Chapter Seventeen

They had barely rejoined the crowd inside when Nash caught Deanna's eye and gave an almost imperceptible nod. She stiffened, swallowed hard and managed a faint smile that was meant to be encouraging. He returned it. For a moment, their eyes met until the experience of looking at him—and the sensations it evoked—became too painful.

Deanna glanced away, blinking rapidly, and reached out blindly to take a glass from a passing tray. She swallowed the contents in a single gulp only to discover too late what it was.

Whiskey. Ah, well, she'd had it before—when her monthlies hurt more than usual or she'd been caught in a dank rain. Whiskey wouldn't hurt her. There were times when it qualified as medicinal.

Such as now. Another waiter passed. She exchanged her empty glass for a full one. Prudently, she took only a small sip as she glanced around.

There was Charles, emerging from his chat with Clinton. He looked well pleased, handsome and confident, as though he hadn't a care in the world. Deanna started toward him. She intended to attach herself to him, the better to forestall any curiosity about Nash's whereabouts.

But before she could do so, Charles caught sight of Edward just leaving the room.

"Nash," he called, "there you are. Don't hurry off. We were just about to catch up on old times." Smiling broadly, he linked his arm through Edward's and led him inside.

Belatedly, Deanna realized that she wasn't the only one who had perhaps been injudicious in the consumption of alcohol. Charles had a decidedly rosy glow, suggesting he'd been imbibing with Clinton and the other officers. The fuzzy cheer of alcohol prompted him to insist on his old school chum's company, not minding that the chum in question was trying his best to extricate himself.

"Not just now, Charles," Nash said. "I really must..."

"By God, that's a fine round of Stilton," Charles said, happily ignoring him as he studied the groaning board. "Remember that night at school when we demolished the proctor's cheese?" Chuckling, he headed toward the table, still linked to Nash.

Deanna bit her lip to keep from laughing, a whiskey induced response that—if the glare Edward shot her was any indication—would not have been well received. Out of the corner of her eye, she saw Clinton and Tyron with their heads together. They were making their way slowly toward the door.

Nash was caught, dragged to the center of the room, with Charles determinedly regaling him about their school days and no hope of slipping away. In a moment, the generals would be gone. Once they were in the meeting room, there would be no hope of slipping in unseen.

Deanna took a final sip of the whiskey, put the glass down, and as casually as she could manage, strolled over to Charles. She put on her best winsome smile, shamelessly batted her eyelashes and took every care not to look at Nash.

Even so, she could feel the heat of his scathing scrutiny, almost as though in those few seconds he had guessed what she was about to do. Before he could say anything to prevent her, she touched her hand to Charles's sleeve and murmured, "I have just a bit of a headache. I'm going to lie down for a while."

Charles broke off in mid-sentence and frowned with concern. "If you're ill—"

"Oh, no," she assured him hastily. "It's merely the excitement. I'm unused to it."

Again she smiled as though to say she was only a woman, after all. Such things were to be expected. He knew that, man of the world that he was. She could count on him to understand. Without hesitation, she gave him a slight shrug of her alabaster shoulders, the merest tilt of her head and a tiny wave of her hand.

Charles understood perfectly. He took her hand, touched it to his lips and said, "There is a retiring room upstairs for the ladies."

Deanna made a little sound, gave him a grateful look and, still avoiding Nash with all her might, slipped away. Once halfway across the room, she speeded up and was just on the verge of running as she reached the hall. Coming to an abrupt halt, she looked around.

Three doors led from the hall. One was toward the back and undoubtedly led to the kitchens. Another gave way to a small parlor in the front of the building. The third, about halfway down, stood open to reveal a small room in the center that looked like little more than an overly large closet. A table was set with a pair of chairs, glasses and several bottles. On a smaller table nearby were several large paper rolls that might have been maps.

Deanna hesitated. People were passing through the hall, coming in and out of the building and the room where the party was being held. She could easily be seen.

Seconds passed. Her throat was dry and her heart beat painfully. She took a deep breath, waiting... waiting.

The hall was momentarily empty. Seizing the chance, she stepped quickly into the small room and went immediately to the closet. If it was full, if there was no room inside, if...

The closet was empty. She darted in and was shutting the door behind her when men's voices heralded the arrival of the generals.

Chairs scraped around the table. Seconds later, the door to the meeting room closed.

* * *

Nash could not believe what had happened. How could such a simple plan go so stunningly wrong? Here he was, trapped, listening to Charles Harrow reminisce about Stilton, of all the bloody things, while Deanna Marlowe—beyond question the most insufferably stubborn female he'd ever had the misfortune to encounter—pulled what had to be the stupidest stunt on record.

Didn't she realize the risk she was running? The odds were overwhelming that she would be caught. Did she imagine she would be able to smile and sigh her way out of trouble? Didn't she know the British were every bit as capable of hanging a woman as they were of hanging a man? Heaven knew, they'd done it before.

His stomach knotted. It was all he could do not to double up his fist and smash it into Charles's smiling face, an action that had as its sole drawback the fact that it would raise too many questions he didn't care to answer.

Charles was still going on about the bloody Stilton. Incredible. Nash hated Stilton and couldn't even remember the incident mentioned, but Harrow seemed to hold it in fondest memory. Now he was starting in on something else . . . a certain establishment in London known for its hospitality to discerning gentlemen . . .

God, how the man could talk. Did he hold silence no virtue at all? Apparently not, for having attracted an audience of appreciative officers who seemed to consider him something of a raconteur, Charles was clearly in his element. Indeed, he seemed to just be getting warmed up.

Nash waited—not something he did well—until at long last Charles appeared sufficiently distracted by his own wit to allow him to slip away. But once out in the hall he hit an immediate snag. Two young stone-faced British officers had positioned themselves in front of the meeting room. Their iron stance said clearly that no one would be allowed to pass.

Cursing under his breath, Nash went outside and skirted the side of the building. Exactly as Fletcher Wesskum had said, the room was windowless. Short of breaking through a wall, there was no way in.

It was a measure of his desperation that Nash actually considered trying to do so. He gave it up when he realized he would only succeed in attracting attention where he least wanted it.

There seemed no alternative but to wait for the meeting to end in the hope that Deanna would somehow manage to escape detection. But once he got her back...

Grimly, Nash set about considering exactly how he would express his displeasure to that stubborn, reckless, maddening young woman. It made him feel a little better, but nothing could ease the stomach-knotting anxiety that dogged him.

Unable to go into the room where Charles was holding court, Nash remained outside. The night was clear and warm. He took a cheroot from the inside pocket of his frock coat and lit it from a silver tinder box he'd had since his school days.

Leaning against the building, he turned the box over in his hand, looking at it absently. There was a small dent in one corner of the intricately carved lid. It had gotten there during a wrestling match with an older boy who tried to take the box from him. He'd kept the box, defending himself and establishing that he was not a good target for the bullying that was a constant part of school life. The grudging respect he'd won had kept him safe enough. He'd even managed to get an education of sorts. But he never lost his contempt for an institution that did nothing to protect the young and weak.

Maybe that had something to do with why he was here, standing under the dark sky in a land torn by war, worrying about a woman he would have preferred just then not to even know. Impatient—with himself, with Deanna and with the entire insane situation—he tossed the cheroot aside and began to pace back and forth.

Time crawled. The strain of doing nothing wore on him. His temper was razor thin and his self control was perilously close to snapping when finally a sudden flurry of activity inside announced that the meeting was over.

Clinton and Tyron emerged, still chatting, and went to rejoin their officers. The two young men who had been on guard duty followed. Seizing the opportunity, Nash entered the room and went directly to the closet. He yanked the door open and plunged a hand inside.

His fingers encountered the petal smooth warm skin of a woman. A whiff of honeysuckle rose tantalizingly. He hesitated, intending to be stern but not quite able to manage it when confronted by such unbridled femininity, such bewitching womanhood, such innocence and passion all wrapped up in—

A snore broke the silence. It was followed swiftly by another. Nash stared in disbelief. Beneath his hand, blissfully unaware, Deanna slept.

Fury shattered the sweet mist of passion. The hours he'd spent agonizing over her safety, the fears he'd had for her, the dreadful possibility of capture, and all the while she'd been *asleep?*

Deanna blinked dazedly. She put a hand up to shield her eyes and peered at him from beneath it. "What...?"

Muttering under his breath, Nash propelled her from the room and down the hall to the outside. He felt her reel back slightly as fresh air struck her. "Breathe deeply," he ordered. "Charles may buy the notion that you fell asleep in the retiring room, but it would be just as well to have your wits about you before you face him. That is, if you have any wits."

Deanna shook her head to clear it and looked at him in bewilderment. "What are you so angry about?" she murmured.

His hand tightened on her shoulder. Unable to stop himself, he shook her. "Angry? Why would I be angry? You think I care that you not only risked your life, you did it for nothing? Maybe you enjoy this sort of thing, but I don't. Go back to Harrow, Miss Marlowe. Marry him as fast as you can and make *his* life miserable. I'm grateful to you for saving mine, but I refuse to put up with you.''

He stopped, thinking that he'd said rather more than he meant but it was true all the same. He simply could not deal with a woman who turned his life upside down the way she did. He was right to say so and to get away from her as quickly as he could. Right to ignore the forest green light of her eyes as they met his or the wry tilt of her delectable lips or the slight shrug of her alabaster shoulders as she said—

''You're such a bear.''

''Bear? I'm no such thing. You're the one who would drive the sanest man on earth to—''

''I only fell asleep at the end,'' she interrupted. Almost casually, as though telling him something he should have had enough sense to know, she added, ''I heard everything they had to say right up to the end when they started talking about somebody named Hortense at a Madam Philoma's in London.'' Her gaze narrowed. ''Do you know her, by the way?''

In fact, the name was familiar but she'd have to rip his heart out before he'd admit it. ''No.''

''Pity, it sounded as though she might be to your taste. I, on the other hand, found her boring and, as it was very warm in the closet, I drifted off.''

If she was toying with him, Nash swore, she'd pay. But first he asked, ''You heard?''

She gave him one small nod. ''Everything.''

"Then we must talk." He took her arm again and began marching off in the direction of the nearest spot he thought might be suitable for such a conversation.

But Deanna was having none of it. She dug her heels in and refused to go.

"Don't be daft," she said. "Charles must be wondering where I am by now. Besides, my father will be expecting me back. We will have to find another time."

Nash hesitated. She was right, damn her, but he hated the idea of letting her go. Nor did he particularly want to examine the source of his reluctance. But the moon was drifting westward, the ball was ending, and at any moment Charles would come looking.

"All right," he said grudgingly. On principal—because he was a man and she a woman, and it did not do for her to forget that too often—he dragged her close against his body, cupped her chin in his hand and, murmuring, "Later," put his mouth to hers.

Chapter Eighteen

"There you are," Charles said. Seeing the direction she had come from, he frowned. "Were you outside?"

Deanna swallowed hard and resisted the temptation to put a hand to her lips. They were still tender from the swift passion of Nash's kiss, which was like a sudden violent storm shattering the night. Clearly, she should have torn herself away immediately. Without doubt, she should not have succumbed even for an instant. Most certainly, she should not have returned his kiss with a fervor that shocked even herself and left him bemused.

The kiss had ended in mutual confusion, leaving them to go their separate ways. He was out there still, somewhere in the darkness, plotting who knows what. But she absolutely wasn't going to think of that. She was going to put him from her mind and concentrate on allaying any suspicion Charles might possibly have.

Forcing a smile, she took his arm. "I needed some

air. Do forgive me. I'm afraid I was quite overcome by all the excitement."

He relaxed and patted her hand. The thought of her as a sensitive female so impressed by a provincial ball as to be done in by it did not seem to strike him as odd in any way.

Deanna repressed a sigh. She had to come to terms with the fact that Charles knew her not at all, nor was that particularly his fault. It was she who had changed, not him.

It was up to her to make the most of his ignorance. Sweetly, she allowed him to hand her up into the carriage. Winsomely, she permitted her hand to remain in his. Docilely, she listened as he rambled on about the evening.

"Good turnout—all things considered," he said. "Can't say I really expected it out here in the wilds."

"Belle Haven isn't exactly the wilderness," Deanna said. "There are some who find it quite civilized."

He laughed as though she had made a particularly witty joke. "That's one of the things that delights me about you. Many women have no sense of humor at all."

In the darkness of the carriage, he could not see her frown. But the tart edge of her tongue was not completely disguised as she said, "London is not the center of the world, Charles. To be honest, I found it dirty, smelly and crowded. In short, overrated."

He turned his head quickly in surprise. "Really? I had no idea. You seemed content enough. Not that it matters, though. I would perfectly understand your desire to remain in the country, especially once children arrive. It's far healthier.''

Her lips could not really be stinging, Deanna thought. They only felt overly tender because her mind insisted on recalling Nash's kiss at that precise moment, comparing him to Charles in a way that was not at all flattering to the Englishman.

Impatient with herself, she resolved to do better, beginning by smothering all thoughts of telling Charles that he was being insufferably presumptuous. She was not about to be relegated to the country with children he had no reason to believe were even going to exist. She attempted to turn his thoughts in a different direction. ''You were with General Clinton for quite a while. He must depend on you greatly.''

Charles modestly forbore from preening but he was clearly pleased. ''Well, without wishing to say too much, I will say he has been most kind.''

''I'm sure he has. Tell me, is he as careful as his reputation claims?''

''Even more so. Caution is his watchword. He is never the first to jump into any situation. He holds back, prudently assessing what is needed before acting.''

Deanna nodded thoughtfully. ''I see, indeed that is wise.'' Her words betrayed her thoughts. Wise, perhaps, for a man with all the time in the world to make decisions, but not for a commander faced with a crisis in which the instant response might be the only one posssible. ''How fortunate he is to have you with him,'' she murmured, hardly aware of what she was saying, so preoccupied was she with thoughts of the British general. Charles's description of him agreed with what she had managed to grasp during his conversation with Tyron. Certainly, the occupier of Belle Haven and the surrounding area seemed by far the more eager to be on about the business of killing and burning, all under the heading of teaching the rebel rabble a long-delayed lesson. Clinton, for his part, seemed more interested in not doing anything that might be later judged a mistake. His reputation concerned him most, not the results he got.

"Patience is called for," Charles pronounced as he moved slightly closer and looked at her intently, "in war as in love."

She was so busy recalling what she had overheard that Deanna didn't realize the sudden change the conversation had taken until Charles's arm slid around her shoulders. She was drawn into his embrace before she thought to act.

Her hand to his chest, she said, "Let us not overstep propriety."

"Propriety be damned," Charles replied. In his sudden ardor, he attempted to press her back against the carriage seat.

Deanna resisted. She shook her head firmly and pushed hard to hold him off. "You forget yourself. We are unchaperoned."

"Your father could have insisted otherwise. He trusts me and that is not misplaced."

"Indeed?" Deanna demanded. Despite her best efforts, she was already halfway down on the seat with

Charles looming over her. The position was fraught with danger, not to mention extremely annoying. "It seems utterly misplaced to me at the moment. My father would be most displeased to learn of this."

Charles did not appear to hear her. His taut features, just visible in the shadows, suggested a man in the grip of an ardor he could barely control.

Genuinely alarmed, Deanna considered the possibility that she would have to defend herself. To do so would certainly force Charles to consider her in a different light, but there might be no helping it.

Cautiously, she began to draw up her knee. His mouth was hot against the curve of her cheek. Distaste coursed through her. In the back of her mind, she marvelled at how she could react so differently to Nash's touch... but that did not bear thinking about just then. "Stop this," she said angrily.

Charles laughed and put his hands to her breasts. That did it. Deanna arched her knee and was about to deliver a telling blow when the carriage suddenly hit a bump.

Charles was lifted several inches into the air, losing his hold on her in the process. She was able to scramble upright. Quickly smoothing her clothes, she glared at him. "Keep away from me."

He paused confusedly, then thrust a hand out to seize her. "Deanna..."

"Your behavior is disgraceful. I don't know what you are thinking of and I don't want to. Kindly keep your distance." She glanced out the carriage window and was relieved to see that they were approaching

Daniels' Neck. "We will be there in a few minutes. I trust you can control yourself at least that long."

Her voice shook slightly. For all her brave words and her justifiable anger, she was also frightened. The sudden display of Charles's passion had brought home to her just how vulnerable she could be. It was an unsettling reminder.

"I'm sorry," he murmured with a note of resentment.

Deanna set her back to him and continued staring out the window until they passed the stone wall and rattled down the lane to home.

She was the first out of the carriage, giving Charles no chance to help her. Without a word to him, she sped up the walk to the door. It opened as she approached.

"There you are," her father said heartily. "Have a good time?"

Not trusting herself to speak, Deanna brushed past him and hurried up the stairs. Behind her, she heard a gruffly voiced question and Charles's stumbling effort to reply.

Chapter Nineteen

Deanna opened the door to her room and stepped inside, shutting it behind her quickly. She leaned against it, her eyes closed, her heart hammering.

Downstairs, she could hear the two men talking but their words were indistinct. Feeling exhausted, she tugged at the ribbon holding her hair and pulled it loose. Her feet hurt. She kicked off her shoes and was just beginning to undo the buttons down the back of her dress when she happened to glance toward her bed.

Deanna gasped. Nash lay there, stretched out full length, dark masculinity against the white lace of her counterpane, a smile on his lips and an unholy light in his eyes.

"Need any help with those?" he asked, looking at the buttons.

"What are you doing here?" Her voice shook. She stared at him in disbelief.

"Waiting for you, of course." He angled himself off the bed in a single motion and walked toward her. His eyes raked her flushed face. "What took you so long?"

"Nothing." Not for the life of her would she reveal what had happened in the carriage, and yet she couldn't shake the horrible thought that he somehow knew. Certainly, he was looking at her suspiciously enough. "Nothing happened," she insisted more emphatically, thinking that in the larger scheme of things, it wasn't really a lie. Nothing of any consequence had occurred except for that regrettable business about realizing that the attraction she felt to Nash didn't extend to other men. No, she had to be drawn to an insufferable, high-handed male who stood there glaring at her as though he was lord of the universe and she was some poor little scrap of humanity who had dared to offend him. The nerve.

"How did you get in here?" she demanded, barely managing to keep her voice down. "You couldn't possibly have gotten past my father. He would have taken your head off. So how did you—"

"The window," Nash murmured. He was smiling suddenly, as though she amused him. "I climbed the tree and came in through the window." For good measure, he added, "If you don't want unexpected visitors, you should keep it shut."

"That hasn't been a problem. *Most* people have the decency not to go where they aren't wanted."

"You mean like into closets to listen to other people's conversations?"

She pressed her lips together hard to hold back the unladylike reply that threatened to spring from them.

After a deep breath, she said, "Never mind. You were crazy to come here. Just go."

"Not until we've talked. This may be our best chance, and there's no time to waste."

A door closed downstairs. There were footsteps in the yard and the sound of carriage wheels. Charles had gone but her father remained. Visions of what would happen if he discovered Nash's presence made Deanna pale. Throwing caution to the wind, she said, "I can meet you later. I'll slip away. You can't stay here. Surely you see that—"

"Hush." His hands closed on her shoulders. Before she could make any effort to stop him, he drew her into his arms and held her gently.

To her horror, Deanna realized that she was trembling. So intense was her fear for him that she could no longer control her reactions. Feeling more vulnerable than she ever had, she lifted her head and looked at him.

Her eyes were wide and luminous, reflecting the silver ribbon of the moonlight flowing through the window. "Please," she whispered, "don't endanger yourself like this. I swear I will meet you as soon as all is quiet. It will be safe in an hour."

In the shadows, his face was hidden but his voice was oddly harsh as he said, "No, it has to be now. Tell me what the generals said."

At her wits' end, terrified that they would be discovered at any moment, Deanna gave up her attempts to make him leave. She could not imagine why he refused but she was done arguing with him. Her only hope now was to get through what she had to say as quickly as possible so that he would go.

"Clinton has received a message from General Cornwallis. Cornwallis believes a decisive battle may be approaching. He alerted Clinton to be ready to ship reinforcements south from New York on short notice."

Nash's hold on her shoulders eased. He dropped his hands and moved away from her slightly. His brows creased. "Indeed? Cornwallis said that, did he? And what was Clinton's response?"

"He suggested to Tyron that he thinks Cornwallis is prone to exaggeration. He said he doubts any battle of real consequence is on the horizon and he expressed some hesitation about removing any troops from New York. He seems to believe they cannot be spared."

Nash stared at her intently. "That's what he said? You're sure?"

Deanna nodded. She didn't understand precisely the significance of what she had heard, but Nash's reaction made it clear he thought it important. "I'm sure," she said. "They went over it several times."

"What did Tyron think?"

She thought for a moment. "I got the impression he didn't want to disagree with Clinton directly but that he wasn't fully in agreement with him, either."

Nash nodded. He turned away, deep in thought.

Deanna waited a moment before touching a hand to his sleeve. Tentatively, she asked, "Is Cornwallis right? Is a major battle approaching?"

"He's one of their better generals. If they were all as good as him, this war would have been over a long time ago."

"And if Clinton fails to support him? What happens then?"

A cold smile spread across Nash's face. "Then all things are possible, sweet Deanna." He fell silent again, but only for a moment. Recalled to his surroundings, he bent slightly and cupped her chin in his hand. Gruffly, he said, "You are a brave woman."

Her throat was tight. She knew without having to be told that it was the highest compliment he could give. Just as she knew that he was going to kiss her and that she wouldn't do a blessed thing to stop him.

His mouth was hard and demanding. She clung to him, her lips parting for the thrust of his tongue. Distantly, her boldness shocked her, but there was no time to be concerned about that. This, she knew, was farewell. In all likelihood, she would never see this man again. But she would remember him forever and remember, too, the hot, sweet longing he awakened in her.

The kiss ended far too soon for both of them. They stood, breathless, looking at each other until a shadow moved in front of the moon. With palpable reluctance, Nash released her and turned toward the window.

Halfway out, a dark shadow against the night, he looked back at her. "Promise me something?"

Anything, she thought. Absolutely anything. The world, the moon, her heart. Anything. "What?"

"That you'll stop taking crazy risks."

A faint laugh broke from her, tinged with tears. "That *I'll* stop? What about you?"

"That's different. I'm a man and you're—"

"I know what I am." She took a breath, summoning patience and endurance for the pain that was already settling over her. On a breath of sound, she said, "I promise."

"Really?" He sounded pleased but surprised.

"If you'll be more careful. Try to miss one or two fights. You don't have to be in them all."

He laughed softly and said, "All right, I'll try."

In silence, she stood, her hands clenched, straining for the last sight of him in the enveloping darkness. Below, the stairs creaked. Nathanial was retiring.

Movement rippled the night beyond the window. "Farewell," the darkness whispered. Tears stung her cheeks. She turned away and shortly crept into a cold and comfortless bed.

Chapter Twenty

An hour later, Deanna gave up the attempt to sleep. She rose, stiff-limbed, and with her white nightgown clinging to her, walked over to the window. Peering out, she saw the landscape wrapped in night, familiar in the way of well-loved things yet subtly transformed from its daytime self. A magical, mysterious place through which she loved to roam.

Even now, as a grown woman, even with the ache deep in her heart. Or perhaps because of it. The night beckoned, warm, sultry, filled with the promise of summer.

She plucked a long, fringed shawl from a drawer and with it over her shoulders slipped on a pair of shoes. Going lightly so as not to disturb her father, she tiptoed down the steps, avoiding the treads that creaked, and stepped from the house.

Moonlight wrapped around her, and drifting wisps of fog whispered over the ground, still warm with the memory of day. She went on unhesitantly, fearless in this place that was uniquely hers. The trees of Daniels' Neck stood sentinel all around her. In the distance, she could hear the sea washing timelessly against the beach.

The air was fragrant with the mingled scents of land and water. Every shadowed rock, every rough-barked tree trunk and spreading branch was well-known to her. She could have walked with her eyes closed through the wood but she went eyes open, drinking in the sights and sounds, the touch and scent of night.

Slim and graceful, proud and strong, she moved through cathedral shafts of moonlight and the ghost-like wisps of fog until she came at last to the moss draped rocks beside the pond.

And there she stopped, head up, breathing in the night as peace stole over her and all the worrying fray of the workaday world slipped from her shoulders like so much forgotten weight.

Slipped, too, like the fringed shawl and white lace nightrobe, falling on a breath of air over the velvet moss. She stood, bathed in silver, her hair tumbling down her back and her skin alive to the sudden, sensual pleasure of the night.

Cool, silken water touched her, sliding over the slender curve of her calves to her thighs, caressing the chalice of her hips and flowing smoothly above her waist to brush lightly at her high, upturned breasts.

She sighed deeply and bent her head back. Floating, drifting as in a dream, she gazed up at the star-speckled sky just visible beyond the branches of the trees. The excitement and dread of the long day slowly eased from her. She felt free and alive. Worry and fear slipped away as though they had never been. She sighed contentedly and turned over, diving smoothly under the water to surface some distance away. Laughing with the sheer pleasure of it, she shook the water from her hair and continued swimming across the moonlit pond.

In the woods beyond, nothing stirred. No breath of air fluttered the leaves, no animal scurried for cover or peered curiously from burrow or branch. There was only silence, broken solely by the sudden harsh intake of breath of the man who stood, his back to an ancient oak, watching the scene before him.

A pulse leaped in Nash's jaw. He stared transfixed, unsure if what he was seeing was real or a figment of his own desires. Hunger flared through him, so raw and intense that it made him gasp.

In the water, silvered by the moon, Deanna hesitated. She turned slightly toward the sound as though suddenly unsure.

Nash moved swiftly into the shadows of the trees. He felt like an intruder, guilty at even so inadvertent an invasion of her privacy, yet unable to turn away. He had stayed behind, delaying his departure to meet again with Fletcher Wesskum. The woodsman, though, had left an hour ago or more, off to the place he kept in the hills, yet still Nash had lingered.

He had told himself it was as well, travel by night was always dangerous. He had what he had come for, and he could afford to wait until morning to make his way. The canoe Fletcher had provided was well hidden in bushes by the shore. It would be there when he needed it.

With luck, he would reach New Jersey the day after tomorrow. From there, it was overland to Washington's headquarters in Virginia, a trip of several days' hard riding. His shoulder still ached. A night's rest would do him good.

Not for a moment did he admit that he was reluctant to leave Daniels' Neck and the woman who dwelled there. Yet now, standing in shadow and moonlight, held rapt by beauty that seemed almost otherworldly, he had to face the truth. Deanna Marlowe held him in thrall as no woman had ever done. Unfledged woman that she was, and infuriating though she could be, he could not free her from his mind.

Or, it seemed, from his body. No hesitation there, no doubt, only raw hunger that made his loins ache and sent his blood running hot and fast with need.

He made a sound deep in his throat, half groan, half curse. His hand, braced against the tree, dug into the bark. Belatedly, he became aware of what he was doing and yanked his hand away, but the damage was done. In the silvered light, he could see the white scar left by his touch.

Angry—at himself, at fate, at the whole infuriating situation—he turned resolutely and began to walk deeper into the woods. He would leave, go his own way, forget what he had seen.

Perhaps he would have had a night breeze not blown over the pond at that moment, setting Deanna to shivering and making her decide that she had been swimming long enough.

Back turned, leaving, Nash heard the sound of water falling, sluicing down long, silken limbs he envisioned all too easily. He stopped, frozen in place, held by the image his wayward mind presented. Slowly, he turned and looked toward the pond.

Deanna had left the water. She stood at the edge, bending slightly as she lifted her clothes.

He stepped toward her, harder than he had to, crunching the dried leaves and pine needles beneath his foot. In the stillness, the snap of a branch seemed as loud as a rifle shot.

Deanna froze. She stood, naked, hair tumbling down her back, the white nightgown clutched in front of her, and stared into the dark woods.

"Who's there?"

He took a breath, drawing it deep into his lungs and letting it out slowly. With it went the best of his resolve, fading into the night. He took one step, and then another, until he emerged from the shelter of the trees and stood looking at her. "You're out late," he said.

Deanna did not move. She made no attempt to flee or even to cover herself. Instead, she looked at him with a kind of inevitability, as though his presence merely confirmed something she had already been thinking. Or hoping.

He didn't care to dwell on that. His life was one of hard practicalities and harsh decisions. So he had survived and so he would continue. There was no room for moon-wreathed maidens and unspoken understandings.

"Put your clothes on," he said harshly. His hands were clenched at his sides. There was a pain in his chest—an empty ache of longing—that was almost beyond bearing.

Still she did not move.

But he did, closer yet, until he stood directly in front of her, so close that he could see the delicate flutter of a pulse at the base of her throat.

"Have you no sense at all?" he demanded. "What were you thinking coming out here like this? And why aren't you running? This is no dream, damn you. It's real." He grasped her shoulders, as though to shake sense into her, but the effort was futile, for he was suddenly, irrevocably swamped by the silken touch of warm, smooth skin and the knowledge, shining from her eyes, that she was not in the least afraid of him.

How could she possibly not be? Was she daft? Or did she perhaps know more than he cared to admit?

Her eyes, he realized, were that impossible shade poised between green and gold. It was a color he had once encountered on a summer day as he stumbled into a forest glen where he found, to his great relief, a cool spring and safety for a time. Leaving the glen, he had looked back, sensing unseen presences that swept all around him, just beyond his touch, yet real all the same.

Unseen, now seen. Beyond touch, now touched. And real, sweet Lord, this woman was the stuff of dreams—yet exquisitely real beneath his hands. Walk away, his better self said. Leave now, go while honor remained and nothing unredeemable had happened.

Moments passed, the space of several heartbeats, and he stayed. The chance to leave, slim though it had been, closed like a door shutting in the night.

He stayed. His eyes met hers, watchful and full of questions. His arms beckoned her to him. She could still halt and go her way.

But she did not. There in the darkness and the moonlight, she moved toward him. His name was on her lips as she let the nightgown fall.

Chapter Twenty-One

Deanna cried out softly. The mossy ground was against her back, Nash moved above her, holding her, shutting out all the world. His callused palms cupped her breasts, his mouth ignited fire down her throat. The rough wool of his breeches slightly abraded her thighs. Slowly, rhythmically, his thumbs moved over her aching nipples, driving pleasure so deep that it pierced her to the quick.

She moaned and grasped his shoulders, not knowing whether to draw him closer or try somehow to push him off. Caught between desire and doubt, overwhelmed by sensations she had never even suspected could exist, she could only cling to him.

He was strength and heat, power and certainty, holding her, touching her, drawing taut every nerve in her body so that her back arched and her body bowed like the string of a harp, exquisitely sensitive to his slightest caress. Breath caught in her throat. His mouth closed around her nipple, tugging gently, evoking a tide of sensation in her. Wave after wave of need washed over her, blinding her to everything but the man above her. She could not be close enough to him. It was impossible to feel enough, give enough, know enough.

He raised his head, gazing down at her. The dark pewter sheen of his eyes held hers. "Deanna . . . ?" It was a whisper, no more, harsh and hoarse. His chest beneath the finely woven linen of his shirt rose and fell swiftly. Heat poured from him. She moved her head against the ground, seeking relief, looking for something she did not understand but could not exist without.

"Nash...please..." She barely recognized her own voice. Who was this passion-caught woman, shorn of pride, stripped to bare emotion? Had this other self been within her all this time, unsuspected, unreleased? On this night and in this place that was uniquely her own, had she been suddenly set free?

He swallowed and she watched the play of muscles down his powerful throat, taking comfort that at least she was not alone. He, too, was caught in passion's crucible, reason shorn.

Emboldened and reassured, she moved her hands down his chest to play at the lace loosely holding the front of his shirt together. Nimble fingers, surprising in their cleverness, made swift work. Swift, too, the reward as they slipped beneath the fabric to find heated skin stretched tautly over powerful muscles.

She gasped, swept by the shock of unrecognition, for this was not herself, but a man who both fasci-

NO RISK, NO OBLIGATION TO BUY...NOW OR EVER!

GUARANTEED

PLAY "ROLL A DOUBLE" AND GET AS MANY AS FIVE FREE GIFTS!

HERE'S HOW TO PLAY:

1. Peel off label from front cover. Place it in space provided at right. With a coin, carefully scratch off the silver dice. This makes you eligible to receive two or more free books, and possibly another gift, depending on what is revealed beneath the scratch-off area.

2. Send back this card and you'll receive brand-new Harlequin Historical™ novels. These books have a cover price of $3.99 each, but they are yours to keep absolutely free.

3. There's no catch. You're under no obligation to buy anything. We charge nothing – ZERO – for your first shipment. And you don't have to make any minimum number of purchases – not even one!

4. The fact is thousands of readers enjoy receiving books by mail from the Harlequin Reader Service® before they're available in stores. They like the convenience of home delivery and they love our discount prices!

5. We hope that after receiving your free books you'll want to remain a subscriber. But the choice is yours – to continue or cancel, anytime at all! So why not take us up on our invitation, with no risk of any kind. You'll be glad you did!

You'll look like a million dollars when you wear this lovely necklace! Its cobra-link chain is a generous 18" long, and the multi-faceted Austrian crystal sparkles like a diamond!

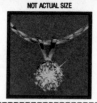

NOT ACTUAL SIZE

nated and frightened her. Fear? A pale thing compared to the curiosity that drove her on.

Daring greatly, she stroked his chest, her palms tingling at the rough caress of down-soft hairs, the remarkable planes and curves so expertly formed, held quiescent yet trembling in their restraint, waiting to be unleashed. It was as if she were touching fire, only she didn't pull away from the singeing heat. This time she went on, unable to stop, drawn by a need vastly greater than any remnant of reason she still possessed.

Nash trembled beneath her questing hands. He rocked with the effort to control himself, long, rolling quakes surging through him. His teeth were clenched, his features strained with the struggle.

She gasped, looking at him, seeing what her thoughtless touch did. "Don't..." she whispered. Fire flashed in his eyes, a wordless message she grasped in an instant. How easily misunderstanding could flare. Her hand moved, coming to rest at his waist. Softly, she said, "I meant don't leave me."

He relaxed slightly but his features were still tight. "You don't know what..."

"I'm saying?" She managed a faint smile. "Perhaps not, but I'm willing to learn."

"This is no joke," he remonstrated. Sternly, he grasped her hands to push her away, but the moment his fingers closed around hers, he hesitated.

She acted on the opportunity. Raising herself slightly, she brushed the tips of her breasts back and forth across his chest. The sensation was enthralling. She had to bite her lip to keep from crying out.

He gasped and, instead of pushing her away, laid her hand against his skin. His eyes closed against the waves of pleasure. Beneath him, lying in the cleft of his thighs, she felt his hardened manhood press against her.

The strength and size of it made her gasp. Trembling on the brink of hesitation, she turned away from that timid edge and suddenly, surprising herself, leapt into the unknown.

Her hands, shocking in their willfulness, touched the waistband of his breeches, undoing the first button and the second. On the third, she paused, and looked at him.

He loomed above her, silhouetted against the darkness, all fire-borne heat and moon madness. Flames flickered in his eyes, flames that darted as he curled his fingers around hers.

"Sweet heaven," he said, half incantation, half simple, male complaint at the mockery of nature that weakens strength and endows the innocent with unmatched wisdom.

In reluctant surrender, he smiled. Rising above her, he stood and quickly stripped off his clothing. The white linen shirt fluttered to the ground. The boots fell with a thud . His breeches followed swiftly and with them his sole remaining garment.

Bathed in moonlight, he stood before her, all sculpted muscle and sinew, raw masculine power and unrelenting will.

Her mouth was suddenly dry. She raised herself on her elbows and glanced around, instinctively seeking some means of escape. But before the thought to flee could fully form in her mind, he came down beside her. Hard hands stroked her from ankle to hip, branding her with his touch. His mouth, hot and demanding, closed over hers devouringly.

Robbed of breath, reason melting, she grasped his shoulders to try to hold herself still in a world swiftly spinning out of control. The effort was futile. The instant she touched him, the last faint bonds of restraint she still possessed snapped.

Crying out his name, she lay back against the earth, drawing him with her. Urgently, she stroked him, caressing the bunched sinews of his back down to his hard buttocks. He groaned and moved a knee between her legs, pushing them farther apart.

"Don't touch me," he said hoarsely. "I want this to be right."

When she tried to protest, he seized both her hands in one of his, and with his fingers twined around her wrist, raised her arms above her head. Darkness stained his lean cheeks. A lock of ebony hair fell across his brow.

"Lie still," he demanded. "Let me do what I must."

Impossible, she thought dazedly, for every touch, every movement elicited such a powerful response from her that she could not help but reach out to him. Her hips lifted, held captive by his caress. Her eyes widened in shock as his hand moved between her legs, stroking the delicate skin of her inner thighs.

"No," she whispered faintly. She was embarrassed yet desperately wanted him to continue. When he did, lightly touching his thumb to the sensitive nub hidden between the folds of her womanhood, she cried out. Waves of ecstasy radiated upward. The night shimmered all around her.

She was hardly aware of what was happening to her, only that he was touching her again, with his hands, with his mouth, and finally with the strong, smooth tip of his maleness.

Poised between her thighs, he lifted her, his fingers kneading her bottom, opening her yet farther. He hesitated a moment longer before lowering his head to hers.

"Sweet," he whispered as he kissed her mouth and thrust his manhood within her.

She stiffened at the stunning intrusion and the swift stab of pain that accompanied it. But both the strangeness and the discomfort fled in an instant, overwhelmed by pleasure so intense nothing else could exist beside it.

He waited, giving her time to become accustomed to him, before he began to move again. Slowly, drawing out each long thrust, he cleaved her body, reshaping her to him while at the same time giving completely of himself.

Undulating ripples of release began deep within Deanna, reaching to the very core of her being. Her head fell back reflecting the silvered sky in her eyes.

Nash grasped her hips, locking her against him. He drove again, once more, again. A throbbing pulse filled them both. Passionately, he cried out her name. The sound seemed to shatter the world and her with it.

Far off, as though in a dream, she soared above the trees, looking down with wonder at herself, joined in such primal beauty with this man. A piercing sense of longing for what could not be filled her.

She held him fiercely to her, willing him never to go. A single, burning tear slipped down her cheek and fell upon the waiting earth.

Chapter Twenty-Two

"No," Nash said. He spoke quietly in the firm manner of one who knows beyond question that there will be no argument. Without looking at Deanna, he added, "I'm going with you."

She stood a little apart from him, dressed once again in the nightgown and shawl. Her arms were wrapped around herself. She looked proud but vulnerable, swamped by emotions he had no trouble recognizing because they were in control of him, as well.

All too quickly, dazzling joy had given way to hard reality. There was no going back from what they had done and no chance of undoing it. Remorse filled him, and with it the hard edge of guilt.

He was the man, vastly more experienced and knowledgeable. He should have known better, should have controlled himself, should have called a halt while there was still time.

Instead, he had surrendered to passion so intense and overwhelming that the memory of it still stunned him. Had it not been for the desire still quickening within his body and the lingering scent of Deanna's skin against his own, he might almost have believed it a dream.

But this was no dream facing him, rather a flesh and blood woman whose eyes shone with bewilderment and what looked perilously like regret.

Pain stabbed through him. He took a step toward her, hoping to somehow offer her comfort and reassurance. But his inner torment surfaced and he spoke far more harshly than he intended. "Don't be a fool."

She winced, but she held her head high and her gaze steady. "It appears I already have been."

Nash froze. Slowly, his hands dropped to his sides. More gently, he said, "It wasn't your fault. I should have known better."

A hint of scorn flashed behind her eyes. Without another word, she turned and began to walk away.

Nash cursed under his breath and went after her. He caught up before she had gone very far but made no attempt to stop her. She was going in the right direction—toward the house. When they were within sight of it, she stopped. Still without looking at him, she said, "Surely this is far enough. Consider your duty done."

She was right, of course. It was madness for him to go any farther. He could remain where he was and watch her until she was safely in the house. Pride refused to let him. He would not let it end like this. The clouds parted suddenly, bathing the edge of the forest where they stood in moonlight. His breath caught as he looked at her. Never had he known a woman so beautiful in every sense of the word, who enthralled not merely his body but his spirit, as well.

A woman he would gladly have swept into his arms and carried away for all time. *If* he had anywhere safe to take her. *If* he could have offered her any life beyond the struggle of war and the ever-present danger of defeat.

Cursing the fate that had thrown them together, he could not resist the impulse to touch her one last time. In the stillness of the wood, with only the moon as a witness, he brushed his hand lightly against her cheek.

It came away damp. He inhaled sharply as pain twisted within him. With a low groan, he drew her into his arms.

She stiffened, and for a moment he thought she would resist. But an instant later, she seemed to melt against him, releasing a soft sigh.

With her head against his chest, she said, "Don't come any farther, please. I'm so afraid you'll be caught."

Nash's throat tightened. He couldn't remember the last time anyone had worried about him like that, had put his well-being first so completely and generously. "I can't leave like this. It isn't right."

Before she could protest further, he set her a little apart from him, took her hand and resolutely moved toward the house. Deanna followed, without objection, but he could feel her trembling.

Directly in front of them, on the lower floor of the house, a light flared. The door to the kitchen opened.

"Someone out there?"

Nash tensed for a moment, readying himself for trouble.

"Martha," Deanna whispered with relief. Loudly, she called, "It's only me."

The door opened farther. Silhouetted against the light, the old woman peered out. "Child, what're you doing wandering around this late? Come inside 'fore you catch your death."

"I must go," Deanna said to Nash. She waited for his response, staring straight at his chest.

Nash took a deep breath, struggling for control. He lifted the delicate hand he still held and studied it for a long moment. Slowly, not looking at her, he said, "I don't want it to be like this."

She raised her head. Her forest-green eyes met his. "But it is and there's nothing we can do about it."

He should be grateful for her acceptance. There was no recrimination, no blame, only a proud, strong woman telling him that she understood the way things were. Her courage made him ache all the harder inside.

He uncurled her fingers one by one, and touched his mouth gently to her palm. A sweet surge of pleasure ran between them before he reluctantly released her.

Still he did not move, but stood tall and dark against the light. Quietly, he said, "If you need to get in touch with me, Fletcher Wesskum will know how."

She looked startled as his words sank in. Her cheeks darkened. There could be more to come from this night than mere memory.

"That isn't necessary," she said stiffly. "I can manage on my own."

He took a quick step closer, the words wrenched from him. "What do you mean?"

"Exactly what I said."

He remembered then what he should not have forgotten, that she was a healer, skilled in the ways of herbs and other remedies, the kind of woman other women turned to for help in delicate matters.

The thought hurt, oddly. He had never been a sentimental man, never thought much, if at all, about home and hearth, a loving wife and children tumbling about her skirts. Indeed, he would have laughed at the notion that such a life held any attraction for him...

Would have laughed. Until now.

Yet what could he say? He could offer her nothing. That failure, more than anything else, robbed him of the right to place demands on her. In the fundamental fairness of his mind, he knew that. But something more primitive than fairness stirred within him, an ancient urge to leave a part of his being behind, safe with this woman.

"Child?" Martha called.

Nash's hand cupped the back of her head. He drew her hard against him, his mouth branding hers in sudden, savage possession. Against her lips, he said, "Send word through Wesskum. Understand?"

Her eyes bright with unshed tears, she wrenched away and moved swiftly toward the door.

For a moment, he saw her there, poised against the rectangle of light. Then the door closed behind her, blocking out the light and leaving him in the darkness.

Chapter Twenty-Three

"It will do you good," Nathaniel said. "I've got to go back to New York and I don't feel right about leaving you here again. Especially not the way you've been acting lately. I'm still worried that you're coming down with something."

"I'm perfectly fine," Deanna said. To emphasize the point, she sat up a little straighter and smiled. They were seated at the oak dining table brought over from England before the war. It was the Sunday after the ball. The windows stood open to admit a soft breeze. Twilight was falling.

Martha, with Deanna's help, had prepared an excellent supper of turbot in white sauce and glazed ham with compote of vegetables. Nathaniel had scraped his plate clean, enjoying it thoroughly. Deanna had eaten little. She'd hoped her father wouldn't notice, but as usual he missed nothing.

Pouring a modest measure of brandy for himself from the carafe on the table, he frowned. "I know you'd enjoy a trip to the city. Thanks to General Clinton, there's still some fine shopping for the ladies there. When was the last time you freshened up your wardrobe?''

"When I had that dress made for the ball.''

He waved a hand, dismissing that. "I meant other things, day dresses, a new riding habit.'' As though coaxing her with a sweetmeat, he added, "Hats. You used to like them and now I hardly ever see you in one.''

"I have several very nice bonnets.''

"What, those old cotton things you wear in the fields? I'm talking about *hats,* girl, those frilly gewgaws with feathers and ribbons.'' He was silent for a moment. "The fact of the matter is I don't think I've been a very good father to you lately.''

"That isn't true. You—''

"Yes, it is. This damn war has me all tied up in knots, but that's no excuse for not doing better by you. You're a beautiful young woman. You need to get out more, have some fun, do the things young people do.''

Deanna hesitated. She loved her father dearly and was touched by his concern but she didn't want to leave him with any misconceptions.

"Does this, by chance, have something to do with Charles?''

Nathaniel shook his head. "No, it doesn't. I got the impression he pushed you too hard and you didn't like it. That's fine. Maybe the two of you will patch things up and maybe you won't. It doesn't matter one way or the other to me. I just want you to be happy.''

Deanna swallowed against the sudden tightening in her throat. "You can say that and still deny that you're a wonderful father?"

Nathaniel looked pleased, if a bit embarrassed. "If you really think I am, I'm glad. But it's still not fair for you to stay cooped up like this. You're coming to New York with me, and by heaven, girl, you're going to have some fun."

Deanna laughed. She couldn't help it. The heavy weight of the past week lifted from her a little. Maybe her father was right. The best thing for her might be to get away. At least in New York she wouldn't be reminded of Nash every time she turned around. She could accompany her father to a few of the parties that seemed to go on constantly in the city, perhaps even do some of that shopping he'd mentioned.

A ripple of feminine pleasure moved through her. "All right," she said. "When do we leave?"

He surprised her. "Tomorrow morning." With a grin, he added, "So you'd better get plenty of sleep tonight. Unless I miss my guess, it might be your last chance for a while."

He was exaggerating, Deanna thought a short time later as she made her way upstairs. They'd have a good time in the city but it wouldn't be like London had been before the war. Then she'd gone through several sets of dance slippers every week and had rarely gotten home before dawn.

New York was, after all, a far smaller city, still clinging to the edge of wilderness. A city that for all its aspirations remained provincial. A larger version of

Belle Haven, really. It would be interesting, to be sure—even entertaining—but it couldn't be expected to be...

Chaos. Absolutely, unbridled chaos. Clutching her skirts around her, Deanna jumped back as a wagon raced past, taking the corner on two wheels. Mud sprayed in its wake, just missing her. She took a breath, trying to steady her nerves, and started to step into the street again only to leap back once more as another carriage dashed past.

"My God," she said under her breath, "who are all these people and why are they in such a hurry?"

Beside her, Nathaniel laughed. "They're New Yorkers, lass. They don't need a reason."

A small opening appeared in the traffic. They hurried across the street, managing to reach the other side just as a half dozen horsemen galloped by. Deanna grimaced, shook the mud from her skirt and said, "It's worse than London!"

"Or better," Nathaniel replied. He stuck his thumbs in his vest pockets and glanced around with a satisfied air. "Depending on your point of view."

"You like it here."

He laughed. "That isn't a sin, lass. It's not a bad place once you get used to it."

"If you say so," Deanna murmured. She didn't try to hide her skepticism. Since their arrival in the city that morning, she'd been bombarded by sights and sounds, not to mention smells, enough to make her head spin. For a city of no more than a few thousand perched on the tip of a largely unsettled island, it had a remarkably self-important air.

Perhaps that was to be expected. The city was headquarters for much of the British force. It had withstood rebel efforts to take it early in the war and remained staunchly Tory ever since, or so it seemed.

As a result, the port stayed busy, people appeared prosperous, and there were no signs of the grim exhaustion that had scarred so many villages and towns during the past five years.

Deanna felt a twinge of envy. She pushed it aside firmly, reminding herself that she was here to have a good time. The sooner she started, the sooner she could get it over with.

"General Clinton's wife is having a little soirée tonight," Nathaniel said. "We've been invited."

Chamber music and conversation with British officers and their wives was not exactly her idea of a rip-roaring evening, but it would have to do. "Wonderful," she murmured as she wondered what she should wear.

It proved easy enough to decide. Until she did the shopping she had promised her father, the only remotely fashionable dress she had was the one made for Tyron's ball.

Dressing that evening in her room in the inn, she did her utmost not to think of Nash. But the touch of silk against her skin and the rustle of the wide skirt as she moved reminded her vividly of that evening and the night that followed.

By the time her father knocked at the door to collect her, she was pale and her hands felt cold. Quickly, she pinched color into her cheeks.

"Lovely," Nathaniel said when she opened the door. With a proud air, he offered his arm. "Now isn't this better than sitting at home with only Lucas and Old Martha for company?"

"They're good friends," Deanna protested.

"Aye, they are, but they want what's best for you, too. General Clinton's lady sets the best table in New York. I hope you're hungry."

Deanna wasn't hungry but she didn't dare say so. Her father seemed happier and more relaxed than he had been in a long time. She wouldn't change that for the world.

The General and Lady Clinton's residence was a pleasant two-story mansion near Canal Street built of native granite and surrounded by a garden and orchard. The house was far grander than Tyron's headquarters in Belle Haven.

Well-dressed men and women were arriving either by carriage or on foot as the Marlowes strolled up. They joined the throng and shortly passed through the high double doors to the entry hall. Deanna yielded her shawl to a majordomo and took her father's arm. They shared a surreptitious smile.

"Remind you of anything?" he asked.

"London," she said promptly. "If I didn't know better, I'd think they transported the entire house from overseas—down to the last peg in the floor and the last bit of molding on the wall."

"The General's lady is said to be a woman of high standards."

"Let me guess," Deanna said. "She wasn't too happy about being sent over here and refused to come unless she could live in the manner to which she was accustomed."

Nathaniel's eyebrows rose. "How did you know that?"

"As I said, a guess. I met ladies like her by the dozen in London. Most thought we went about half naked, ate our meat raw and slept in trees."

"And those were the ones who were trying to be nice to you," a voice said lightly.

Deanna whirled to find Charles close beside her. In the press of the crowd, she hadn't noticed his approach. Now, it was impossible to ignore him.

With a cautious smile in her direction and a bow to Nathaniel, he said, "I heard you might be coming this evening."

"Did you?" her father murmured. "I didn't know myself until we got the invitation earlier today."

Charles flushed slightly. He stood with his hands tucked behind his back, resplendent in his dress uniform. "Actually, I asked Lady Clinton to send it."

"Very resourceful of you," Nathaniel said dryly. He glanced at Deanna and inclined his head toward the music room. "The music seems to be starting."

Charles followed as they moved inside. He took a seat next to Deanna, carefully spreading the tails of his frock coat before lowering himself into the chair.

Staring straight ahead, he said, "I hope I'm not being presumptuous."

She lowered her eyes to hide the anxiousness in them. The situation appalled her. She had known she would most likely encounter Charles during this trip, but she hadn't expected it to happen so soon or for him to make his continued interest in her quite so clear.

She could hardly tell Charles that there was no point in his sitting next to her or doing anything else, so far as she was concerned, because she had irrevocably given herself to another man, one she would probably never even see again. He would think her mad. She had to wonder if he wouldn't be at least a little right.

At a complete loss as to what to say or do, she was suddenly grateful for the childhood etiquette lessons that had been so tiresome at the time but at least had given her something to fall back on when she needed it most.

"Do you enjoy this sort of music?" she asked politely.

If he was surprised by the indirectness of her reply, he gave no sign. With a grave nod, he said, "Upon occasion. And you?"

"The same."

The first notes of the harpsichord relieved them of any further need for conversation. With a small sigh of relief, Deanna settled herself to listen.

Chapter Twenty-Four

Her relief was short-lived. All too soon, it seemed, the music ended temporarily and people began to circulate. A literary light—a poet from London—was holding court in the parlor. Charles suggested Deanna might find him interesting.

Father and daughter exchanged a glance. There were people Nathaniel wanted to talk with, men like himself anxious to do business despite the difficulties imposed by the war. He had returned to New York for that opportunity. She could not bring herself to deny it, no matter how uncomfortable she might feel.

Giving her father a reassuring smile, she touched the tips of her fingers to Charles's arm and accepted his escort. With the poet, Lady Clinton was also in the parlor. She was a plump woman tightly laced into an extravagant gown of ruffles and bows, her powdered wig framing noble features. She gave Charles a chiding look as he came up to present Deanna.

"There you are, sirrah," Her Ladyship said. "Do

remind me, when was the last time you graced one of my little dos?"

Charles flushed but kept his composure. "Alas, madame, duty too often calls me away."

"Nonsense, you simply prefer the gaming tables and pleasure parlors, like most of the men in this dreadful place." Belatedly noticing Deanna, Her Ladyship added, "Do forgive me for being blunt, dear, but the longer we are forced to remain here, the more difficult it becomes to maintain one's standards. Don't you agree?"

Neatly put on the spot, Deanna debated what to say. The proper response was to defer to her hostess, but the plain fact was that she wasn't feeling particularly deferential. Indeed, the general's wife's arrogance struck a nerve in her that she couldn't ignore.

"No, actually I don't," she said quietly. Beside her, she felt Charles stiffen. "But then, I'm American, so it's only natural that I would be more comfortable here than you."

Lady Clinton's rather small eyes widened visibly. She stared at Deanna as though she were some strange species of creature who had suddenly crawled out of the carpet. "I beg your pardon?"

"There is good to be found everywhere," Deanna said softly. "You might be happier if you looked harder."

"Why, I never—"

"We've kept you from your other guests long enough," Charles said, stepping in hastily. With a firm grip on Deanna's arm, he added, "If you'll excuse us—"

Not waiting for Her Ladyship's approval, he steered Deanna away. When they were out of earshot, he demanded, "What in God's name did you think you were doing? Next to Cornwallis, Clinton is the most important representative of the King on this continent. He also happens to be my commanding officer. Yet you just took it upon yourself to insult his wife. Why?"

Deanna was wondering that herself. It was unlike her to be rude in any situation, much less one that was so public. Yet she'd done exactly that. Apparently, her nerves were more frayed and her emotions more perilous than she had realized.

"I'm sorry," she said with quiet dignity. "It's only that she was being so insufferable. I've been to London. Contrary to what some people seem to think, it's not heaven on earth. There's dirt and noise and poverty and violence, just as there is here. That's the problem with you British. You honestly believe you're superior to everyone else and that everything you have is better than what any of the rest of us can even hope for. But that just isn't true."

It was difficult to say who was more surprised by her outburst, Deanna or Charles. She was taken aback by the force of her convictions, hitherto little thought about, and by the frankness with which she had suddenly expressed them. For his part, Charles gave every appearance of being stunned. He stared at her in amazement.

"How long have you felt this way?"

"I don't know. Not long. I didn't used to think much about it, but lately..."

"Lately, something has happened to change you."

Her head shot up, her eyes meeting his. He couldn't possibly know. She looked the same as she always had, she was even wearing the same dress he had last seen her in. The transformation in her, born of moonlight and passion, was secret, hidden, not something that could be seen.

Or was it? Was there some sign, perhaps not truly visible, but enough to trigger a male instinct?

"Not something for you to be concerned with," she said quickly. That was the truth. Even if there had been any hope of a future between them, which she strongly doubted, having given herself to Nash, she would never under any circumstances attempt to trick or deceive Charles.

She understood full well without having to be told that virtue was an absolute requirement in anyone he would take to wife. That she felt no regret at having removed herself from the running told her forcibly that her feelings for him had never been deep enough. They were both better off, but he did not realize that and she was in no position to explain it.

"All things regarding you concern me," Charles said. He did not look happy about it. Still holding her arm, he led her farther off to the side in the direction of French doors. Several of the doors stood open to admit a cooling breeze. Beyond them was a stone terrace that gave way to the garden.

"Let's get some air," Charles said.

"I really don't—"

His hold on her arm was suddenly painful. Through clenched teeth, he said, "Stop arguing. I don't remember you being this contentious in London."

"That was five years ago," Deanna protested. Short of making a scene, there was nothing she could do to stop him from leading her out of the parlor and onto the terrace. A scene was undoubtedly just what Lady Clinton would have liked, the certain guarantee that any possible romance between a promising officer and the young woman she now had every reason to dislike would be finished for good. That satisfaction Deanna would not give her, not even with the little voice in the back of her mind warning that such stubbornness might be shortsighted.

However annoyed he might be, Charles was a gentleman. He would find a scene no more to his liking than she did. He might voice his disapproval, but surrounded by fellow officers and other people of stature, he would not go any further. A few minutes on the terrace with him were not so great a risk, and besides, she would slip away the first chance she got.

But Charles did not even pause on the terrace. He yanked her down the few steps to the garden and strode toward the shadows of the nearby orchard. Before Deanna could attempt to stop him, they were alone, out of sight and beyond earshot of anyone.

Chapter Twenty-Five

"I have tried to be patient," Charles said. "We have been apart for five years and it was inevitable that you would have changed to some degree. But now I see that I did not fully appreciate the strain you have been under. A woman's mind is naturally weak. You cannot be expected to think clearly under difficult circumstances."

It was Deanna's turn to be taken aback. She had grown up in a family where her intelligence and general good sense were taken for granted. To the best of her knowledge, no one had ever seriously questioned them. Nor had Charles given any sign that he thought her simpleminded in those long-ago days in London. She was tempted to congratulate him on having so effectively pulled the wool over her eyes. But sarcasm required more effort than she was willing to muster.

Angrily, she said, "I am sorry to hear that you feel that way. Since I cannot abide a man who thinks me a dolt, this would seem a logical time for us to take our leave of one another. Goodbye." Turning on her heel, she picked up her skirts and walked briskly toward the manor house. She got perhaps a half dozen yards before Charles caught up with her.

He grasped her shoulder harshly and spun her around. His eyes were furious, his features taut. There was a slight tremor to his mouth.

"No one turns on me like that. You embarrassed me in front of the general's lady. We will go back inside and you will apologize, or by God, you will regret it."

"I regret nothing except mistaking you for a reasonable man. Now let go."

Instead, his hand tightened. She had the sudden, frightening realization of having gone too far. His free hand rose to strike her.

There was a sudden burst of noise and laughter from the house. Charles hesitated a scant instant. It was enough. Deanna wrenched herself free and ran. Her heart was pounding so loudly that she could not hear whether he was following her or not. Out of breath and genuinely terrified, she reached the terrace and darted quickly inside. Several people looked at her curiously. She brushed past them and, still shaking, made her way upstairs to a cloakroom.

It was, thankfully, empty. She was able to sink down on the couch and try to collect herself. The magnitude of her own misjudgment was just beginning to register. Even after the episode in the coach, she still hadn't realized how insistent Charles could be or what his pride might drive him to do. He would make a bad enemy.

Shakily, she rose and poured water from a ewer on a nearby table. Bathing her face and wrists made her feel a little better. But the mirror over the basin revealed a young woman with strained, pale features and shadowed eyes. She could not let her father see her in such a state. He would surely ask questions she did not wish to answer.

Hearing feminine voices approaching, she slipped out of the cloakroom and looked around for somewhere she might rest undisturbed for a short while longer. No place immediately presented itself until she noticed a door standing open farther down the hall.

Quickly, she stepped inside, finding herself in a small but graciously furnished bedroom. By the look of it, and the lack of any personal objects, it appeared to be kept for guests. With a sigh, she sat down on the edge of the bed, being careful not to wrinkle the counterpane, and looked at her feet.

Her slippers were ruined, damaged beyond repair by the trek in the orchard. She would have to conceal them from her father, who would know beyond doubt that she had not destroyed them dancing. It would be one more lie and deceit among what had already become too many.

Tears stung her eyes. She blinked them back furiously and tried to decide what to do next. She had to go downstairs, find her father and wait patiently until he was ready to leave, concealing from him any hint of what had happened. For the moment, that seemed beyond her. She remained where she was.

Only gradually did she become aware that she was not alone. A soft murmur of voices reached her. She started and looked around quickly. There was no one in sight, yet the voices seemed nearby.

Puzzled, she got up and began moving around the room. At first, she thought she must be hearing people next door. But an ear to the wall proved this wrong. Minutes passed before she noticed the fireplace. A quick check revealed that the flue was open. When she bent closer, the voices became more distinct. They sounded as though they were coming from directly below, filtering up the chimney that must also serve a fireplace in a room beneath.

As nearly as she could make out, there were two men talking. They sounded relaxed and in good humor. One of the voices was vaguely familiar. It took her a moment to realize that it belonged to General Clinton.

A faint smile touched her lips. She seemed to have a talent for this eavesdropping business. All the same, she had been raised with certain standards of courtesy. Turning to go, she froze when a single word caught her ear.

"Traitor."

"Harsh, don't you think?" Clinton asked. "After all, he's doing us a great service."

The other man murmured something Deanna could not make out, then added,

"I suppose we should be grateful. Still, it gives me pause. That sort of thing shouldn't be necessary."

"It wouldn't be," Clinton replied, "if these Americans didn't have the devil's own luck. They should have been defeated long ago. Now there actually appears to be a chance they could win."

"The hell you say. Bunch of rabble, that's all. If it weren't for the French helping them—"

"They would still be a problem. Face it, my friend, we need any edge we can get. We're fortunate to have an agent in their camp." Clinton chuckled. "Particularly when he's managed to convince them that he's actually working for them."

"Still leaves a bad taste. Not the sort of thing either of us would do."

"But then we don't have to," the general replied. "We have him."

The other man agreed, reluctantly. A few moments later, their voices grew fainter. They appeared to have left the room, undoubtedly rejoining the party.

Deanna remained where she was, frozen in place. What had struck her as amusing at first—her unexpected penchant for eavesdropping—was now anything but. Completely by accident, she had come into possession of information that might be vital to the Americans.

The only question was what to do with it.

Chapter Twenty-Six

Hours later, alone in her room in the inn, Deanna considered her options. They were distressingly limited. If she had been in Belle Haven, she could have turned to Fletcher Wesskum for help in contacting the Americans. But he was miles away, and she was surrounded by British loyalists. There was no one to confide in and nowhere to turn.

She was badly frightened, a sensible enough reaction. But she was also oddly exhilarated. Far too much to sleep. Curled in the window seat, her knees drawn up to her chin, she gazed out at the road immediately beyond the inn.

All day long, wagons, carriages, riders and pedestrians had moved along it. But now it was still. Even the noises that had been coming from downstairs were gone, the last of the diners and drinkers departed.

Immediately next door, her father slept. A stout wooden bar secured her door. The bed was clean and comfortable, a rarity in such places. There was nothing to prevent her from seeking the rest she so badly needed. Nothing except the turmoil of her thoughts.

Unbidden, the memory of Nash rose to torment her. She made a small, pained sound and turned away from the window. With the wane of day, the air had grown chill. The thin nightgown she wore offered scant protection.

Going over to the clothes-press, she hesitated before reaching inside. Her hand emerged clutching a dark, elegantly tailored frock coat. Shivering, she wrapped herself in it and lay down on the bed.

It was foolish to be doing this, but she couldn't seem to help herself. The soft wool still held the fragrance of leather and woodsmoke, crisp soap and night air, all so powerfully reminiscent of the man who had placed it around her shoulders. Enveloped in the remembered scent and touch of him, she finally drifted into restless sleep.

It was morning when she awoke. The street outside was once again filled with noise, and her father was knocking at the door. "Deanna," he called, "are you all right?"

She rose hastily, only just remembering to hide the frock coat under the bedcovers. Seizing an extra blanket, she wrapped it around herself and opened the door.

"I'm fine," she murmured groggily. "What's wrong?"

Her father's face was strained with worry. "I've been trying to wake you," he said. "You didn't answer."

A stab of guilt went through her. "I'm sorry. I must have been sleeping more deeply than usual. Is it very late?"

He relaxed somewhat now that he could see that she was really fine. "Not terribly. There's still plenty of time for breakfast."

She flashed him a quick smile. "Good, I'm starved. I'll get dressed and join you downstairs."

Nathaniel nodded, satisfied that all was as it should be, and left. Alone, Deanna shut the door and leaned against it, struggling for calm.

The night's rest—if it could be called that—had done her little good. She felt weighed down by apprehension, her nerves strung taut as though they sensed some calamity about to occur.

But nothing did happen as she dressed and joined her father below. They shared a hearty breakfast of porridge laced with honey washed down by cider. Despite her concern, Deanna did justice to the food. She was young and healthy, after all, and she'd eaten nothing the night before. Besides, she'd always liked porridge.

"Seems like you were right," her father said as they left the inn. "You are fine. Now about that shopping—"

She sighed and pretended to hesitate. "Do I have to?"

"Sure do. I've got to meet with my factor this morning, but there's some real nice shops right by his office. I expect you to go into each and every one of them."

"I suppose it doesn't cost anything to look."

"No, but it does to buy." He took a heavy sack of coins from his pocket and dropped it into her hand.

Deanna gasped. She didn't have to open the sack to know that it contained a good deal of money. "You're not serious."

"I am. We've been hoarding every penny since this damn war started. I'm sick of it. It's time we forgot about the troubles and enjoyed ourselves a little."

"This isn't a little," she protested. "There's enough here to choke a horse."

Her father laughed. "I'm sure you can find a better use for it. Spread it around real good. I don't want to see a bit of it coming back."

"I'd have no idea what to buy." She couldn't remember the last time she'd gone shopping. Suppose she'd forgotten how?

"You can start right here," Nathaniel said, gesturing at the shop nearest to them. "There's a nice lady who's just waiting to make you up a bunch of pretty dresses. Oh, and don't forget that new riding habit I mentioned. Tell her you need that first."

"Why on earth would I need a new riding habit? When people in Belle Haven go hunting, they do it on foot and with a gun. I'll never wear the thing."

Nathaniel lifted his eyes heavenward as though beseeching the Almighty for patience. "We should have stayed in England longer. Maybe then you'd know riding habits aren't just for hunting in. You wear them to... well, to ride in so as other people will know that you know what's what."

"So?"

"So day after tomorrow there's going be a promenade right through the city streets and all the way up to Greenwich Village where the merchant's guild will be hosting a very nice luncheon outdoors, complete with music and fine food. We'll be there."

Deanna frowned. She knew she'd slept badly and had all sorts of things on her mind, but this wasn't making any sense. "Isn't this a strange thing to do in the midst of a war?"

"That's the point. General Clinton thinks it's important to show confidence at this stage."

"And what do you think?"

Her father was silent for a moment. His smile had gone. Quietly, he said, "That's British sterling I gave you. It's been legal tender here for as long as any of us have been around. But maybe we should be getting something for it while we still can."

Deanna took a quick breath. Unless she was mistaken, her father had just told her that he thought there was actually a chance the British might lose the war.

Several soldiers walked past them. There were more up and down the street, as well as numerous civilians. It was impossible to speak without the risk of being overheard.

Since she now considered herself something of an expert on hearing conversations that were not as private as people imagined them to be, Deanna was inclined to be cautious. Still, her father's sudden revelation demanded some response.

"A riding habit?" she asked. "Hats and dresses? Are those things we really want?"

He smiled down at her, his eyes suddenly tender. "I want you to have them and you can't tell me that deep down inside you don't want that, too."

"What about seed stock? A new plow? Medicines, bolts of sturdy cloth, things we're really likely to need if you're right—"

He touched a finger lightly to her lips, stilling her. Softly, he said, "Sweet girl, I thought you understood. If the worst happens, there'll be no place here for men like me, those who stayed on the side of King and Country. We'll have no choice but to leave."

Deanna's breath caught. Standing on the busy street, surrounded by anonymous passersby, she felt as though her world had shattered. Her father had just calmly told her that he was actively considering the need to leave Belle Haven.

The thought tore at her. She had a sudden, wrenching vision of the well-loved house on Daniels' Neck slipping away from her as though down a long tunnel into oblivion. "No, you can't mean it."

Her father laid a hand on her arm in warning. "Calm yourself. This is not the time. I'm sorry to upset you but I thought you knew." He shook his head. "I've been remiss. We will talk more later."

He gave her a small push in the direction of the shop. "Go on now. Enjoy yourself and don't worry about anything. It'll all take care of itself in the end, whatever we do."

Dazedly, Deanna obeyed. She entered the shop, presented herself to the proprietress and recited her needs. What she said must have made sense, for she was quickly shown to a chair where she could comfortably consider the bolts of cloth brought for her examination.

Three hours later, she emerged having ordered a sizeable enlargement of her wardrobe and secured the promise that the riding habit would be ready on time. Deanna couldn't imagine how the garment could be ready on such short notice, but she presumed it had something to do with the exorbitant price she was paying for it.

Anything else to do with her purchases had passed her in a blur. If pressed to describe what she had ordered, she would have been at a complete loss. She could only trust that the garments would be suitable.

But for what exactly? Exile in England? Her stomach tightened in rejection. If her father was right, the information she had gleaned about the traitor in the American ranks might be more essential to the rebels than ever. But if she made any move to help them beyond what she had already done, she might only be assuring the loss of the one place on earth she held dearer than any other. The only place she could call home.

Yet surely she had no right to put her own interests above those of an entire nation struggling to be born. And what of her brother, gone to aid the cause? And Uncle Duncan and his boys? What of the brave people of Belle Haven who had suffered all these years because they wouldn't swear loyalty to a King they believed had abused them? What of Nash?

Grimly, she thrust the thought of him aside. Her emotions were too fragile, her course too uncertain. If she allowed herself to dwell on him, she would be lost for certain.

She crossed the road and walked a little way down to a bookstore she had noticed earlier. It wasn't yet time to meet her father. Having done his bidding, she sought now to indulge her own. The shop was small but surprisingly well-stocked. Barely had she opened the door than the fragrance of leather bindings and crisp, uncut pages rose to welcome her.

The shopkeeper was in the rear. He called out a greeting but left her to her own devices. She picked up a small volume of poetry and began to peruse it.

The door opened again. She lifted her head idly as a bewhiskered captain entered. He nodded and continued on toward the back. Behind him, a fragment of the street was framed in the half-open doorway. Deanna was returning her attention to the book when she noticed a horseman passing by.

The door was swinging shut. It closed even as she took a quick step forward, telling herself she must surely be mistaken. The man she had just seen couldn't possibly be Nash. He was supposed to be with General Washington in Virginia. Not here in New York on the very doorstep of the British! Her eyes had to be playing tricks on her.

Chapter Twenty-Seven

Two days later, Deanna had all but forgotten about the man she thought she had seen. She was far too busy with fittings, more shopping and visits to her father's merchant friends to have any time to dwell on the matter. In what spare moments she could find, she tried to come up with a way to contact the Americans. But any possibility of that continued to elude her.

On the second day, she woke early and began to dress with special care. Nathaniel had procured two fine mounts for them to ride in the promenade. She wanted him to be proud of her.

The seamstress arrived with her riding habit shortly after breakfast. Dark shadows under the woman's eyes testified to the effort needed to ready the garment so quickly. But she was clearly pleased with the results, not to mention her own reward.

"You look lovely, miss," the woman said after she had helped Deanna on with the burgundy wool and velvet habit. The shade was well-suited to her coloring, and the snug fit of the jacket emphasized the feminine curves of her breasts and waist.

With only a small mirror to look in, Deanna couldn't really judge for herself. But she was content to take the seamstress's word for it. She thanked the woman warmly and assured her that it would be fine to send the other clothes on to Belle Haven when they were ready.

The seamstress gave her a grateful smile and took her leave. Deanna spent a few minutes fixing her hair. She couldn't abide wigs and had no patience with the stuffed and powdered artifices that were all the rage. It was enough to coil part of her heavy, golden tresses high up on her head, leaving a gleaming length to fall beneath the pert, feathered cap that matched the habit.

Confident that she would do her father proud, she left the room and descended the stairs to find him waiting for her below. Her heart tightened as she caught sight of him. Although in his fifties now, he was still a fine figure of a man.

All her life he had been there to catch her when she fell, dry her tears and assure her, often without words, that she was an important and valued person worthy of being loved. She had come to take him for granted, as children had a way of doing.

But in the last few days, she had been forced to confront the possibility that their lives would take them in very different directions. If the Americans won and her father chose exile in England, she would have to decide whether or not to go with him. The thought that she might not was like a knife blade running through her, agonizing and impossible to ignore. Yet she could say nothing of it to him, not by the slightest word or look could she hint at what she was thinking. It would hurt him too deeply. With a quick smile, she took his arm.

Softly, he said, "You look absolutely lovely."

"Must be the company I keep." With a flutter of her skirt, she stepped out into the sunlight.

The riders assembled near the Bowery, almost at the tip of the island, and with much cheering and laughing began to proceed up the broad way. Beyond the old city walls built by the Dutch, they spread out, following the tracks of what had been hunting paths or the shallow beds of streams.

The day was fair, the sky cloudless and the breeze just brisk enough to cool brows heated by the excitement. Up ahead, Deanna caught a glimpse of Lady Clinton resplendent in a black riding habit trimmed with ermine. The general accompanied her, surrounded by a group of his officers. Charles was among them.

He saw Deanna and frowned. His eyes lingered on her as he appeared to debate whether or not to approach her. Discretion won out and he kept his distance, for which she was grateful. But from time to time, she felt him looking at her.

Determined not to let anything spoil the day, she did her best to ignore him and to a certain extent succeeded. She had always enjoyed riding, but in recent years there had been little opportunity to do so for pleasure. Now she gave herself up to it, listening idly to the conversation of her father and his friends but otherwise letting her thoughts drift.

Shortly after noon, the road widened again as the party approached the village of Greenwich. People came out to welcome them, the children shrieking in excitement while the adults waved and called out greetings.

Wryly, Deanna thought no one coming upon such a scene would think for a moment that this was a country at war. And that, she knew, was precisely the point. Clinton was determined to show that the population was utterly loyal, so much so that he could relax and enjoy himself as well as any squire at home in England. He meant to put the lie to claims that the rebels were gaining not only in the field but also in the hearts of the people.

But was he right? Here and there, she thought she caught glimpses of faces that did not appear so happy. Eyes shadowed by unspoken thoughts. Mouths set with grim determination.

Perhaps she was imagining it. Everyone seemed cheerful enough around the large tables that had been set up on the village green. White linen cloths billowed in the breeze as liveried waiters stood by to serve the guests.

"Extraordinary," Nathaniel murmured under his breath. "We could be on someone's country estate with no more to be concerned about than whether the rain was going to hold off."

"The general apparently likes to enjoy himself," Deanna said mildly.

Her father made a disapproving sound. "Maybe too much. Someone might need to remind him that we're at war."

"Of course, he didn't actually arrange this. The merchants did."

Nathaniel scoffed. "Because they believe what he tells them." He shook his head as though exasperated. "Damned if I can understand it. I've known most of these men for years. They used to be as sensible as the day is long. But they seem to have bought Clinton's notion that the Americans can't win."

Deanna laid a warning hand on his arm. His voice had risen slightly, enough to attract the attention of several people nearby. "This may not be the place."

He sighed but relented. More softly, he said, "You're right. Besides, I don't want to spoil your outing. Shall we stroll around a bit before getting something to eat?"

Deanna allowed as to how that would be very nice. She took her father's arm and glanced around. "This seems a pretty place."

Nathaniel nodded. "Good duck hunting nearby." He smiled wryly. "You know, there are some who say the city's going to grow so fast that eventually this little village will be in the thick of it."

"But that would make it huge—as big as London."

"Hardly likely."

Putting aside the notion of a city grown vastly beyond its present confines, they set out across the green.

Before they could get very far, Nathaniel encountered an acquaintance, a fellow merchant whom he'd not yet had a chance to converse with. After introducing Deanna, he quickly fell into a discussion of the trade outlook in the coming year.

Left to her own devices, she watched a group of children playing with a wooden ball, hitting it back and forth across the green with sticks. Their eager energy reminded her of herself at that age. She was caught up in the pleasure of remembered pastimes when the ball suddenly shot past her and vanished into the trees behind where she was standing.

The children were still some distance away. "I'll get it," she called and turned toward the wood. The ball had rolled into the underbrush. She had some trouble finding it. In the process, her hat was knocked askew by a low branch and her skirt caught on some brambles. Finally, she came up laughing, the ball in her hand. Only to find that she was no longer alone.

A tall, powerfully built man leaned against a nearby tree. His arms were folded over his broad chest, his long legs crossed indolently. He wore black from the tips of his highly polished boots to the severely tailored frock coat stretched over his wide shoulders. His eyes gleamed as he surveyed her. Huskily, Nash asked, "How is it, Miss Marlowe, that I keep finding you where you aren't supposed to be?"

Chapter Twenty-Eight

"You," Deanna said. She took a quick step backward. Her foot caught in the underbrush and she lost her balance. With an undignified *umph* she landed on her posterior.

Nash sighed and held out a hand. She ignored it and scrambled to her feet, still holding the wooden ball.

"Did you find it, lady?" a young voice called. The bushes parted to reveal three worried-looking children studying her.

"Here," she said, and tossed it to the smallest.

He caught it with a grin and raced off whooping, the others in hot pursuit.

Task completed and in haste to depart, she gave her skirt a quick twitch, nodded curtly to Nash and said, "I must rejoin my father."

"He seems happy to be debating coffee futures with several gentlemen."

Her eyes widened. "You spoke with him?"

"Only in greeting. He looked as though he thought he ought to recognize me but couldn't quite manage it."

"Thank heaven for that." She started as Nash stepped closer. Gently, his long, blunt fingers brushed a stray leave from her cheek.

"Your hat's on crooked."

She flushed and tried to ignore the sudden torrent of sensation his touch set off in her. She refused to meet his eyes. "It's supposed to be like that."

Nash frowned, looking doubtful. "If you say so. Now suppose you tell me what brings you to New York?"

It was on the tip of her tongue to tell him it was none of his business and good-day, but she had no actual reason to be rude to him, and besides, she knew perfectly well he wouldn't allow her to get away with such an answer. All she would succeed in doing was prolonging the encounter. She refused to admit to herself that she might want to do exactly that. "I'm accompanying my father. Now I really must—"

"Is that the only reason?"

She shook her head, puzzled. "What do you mean?"

"Not the redoubtable Charles."

Despite herself, Deanna winced. "Good lord, no."

Nash's smile was insufferably self-satisfied. Also savagely attractive, damn the man.

"Just thought I'd check. So are you enjoying yourself?"

"No, I'm not. For one thing I'm being kept here standing in damp underbrush under circumstances that at any moment could attract suspicion. So if you don't mind, I'll—"

She stopped short and stared at him. Perhaps it was the lack of sleep in recent days or more likely the sheer confusion he induced. But there he was, the answer to her most recent prayers, and she hadn't even realized it.

"Nash," she said suddenly, "we really must talk."

He frowned again, understandably enough given her swift change of mood. Poor male, he had no insight into it at all and promptly leapt to the wrong conclusion.

"About what?"

"A matter of great importance. But not here, it isn't private enough. We must meet somewhere."

His frowned deepened. "Do I understand you? We have something of a private nature to discuss that's important?"

"Yes, but—"

The sudden dark flush that suffused his cheeks was her first clue. The flare of light in his silvered eyes was the second. His hands reached for her. In an instant, she was drawn into his arms and gently soothed.

"Dear girl, everything will be all right. Believe me."

Deanna groaned. This was really too much. There she stood, torn between the exquisite pleasure he unleashed with infuriatingly little effort and the dreadfully serious business they needed to discuss. And all the while, he was off on some grand conclusion of his own that only too vividly reminded her of what had happened between them. "Not that. For heaven's sake, I wouldn't even have time yet to know."

Her frankness startled him, enough so that he dropped his hands and stepped back to get a better look at her. "Are you sure?"

"Yes." she was struck by the suspicion of disappointment lurking in his eyes. What a baffling man he was. "I overheard something else," she went on hastily, "at another party General Clinton attended. I'm afraid it may be—"

"Deanna," he interrupted, "you haven't been going around playing spy, have you?"

She bristled at the notion. "Certainly not. I simply happened to be in a certain place quite accidentally." He looked unconvinced—and disapproving. "I am hardly to be blamed if voices travel up a chimney and if flues are left open when they shouldn't be. At any rate, do you want to hear this or not?"

"Of course I do, but—"

"Deanna?" Her father's voice erupted, sounding close by and worried.

"Damn," she muttered. "We can't talk here."

"I'll find you," he said quickly and gave her a little shove. "Go on."

She went but not without glancing once over her shoulder. Nash had vanished into the woods. Only the lingering sensation of his touch on her skin assured her he had been there at all.

* * *

The party on the green in the midst of the village of Greenwich reminded Deanna of something, but she couldn't quite place it. Late afternoon sunlight filtered through the tree branches before she remembered.

During their visit to England, she and her father had been invited to a ball at the country residence of distant acquaintances. The occasion had more than lived up to her imaginings. For three days, several dozen guests were entertained by every sort of amusement as well as the finest food and drink. The gaiety seemed unending, and yet it had also seemed oddly strained.

By the end of the visit, the hosts' ceaseless race to the next diversion, the next pleasure, the next extravagance had taken on a frantic quality that disturbed her. When the time came to depart, she was exhausted and glad to be leaving.

Barely had she and her father returned to London than word reached them that their host and hostess had fled to the continent. Unable to pay their debtors and with their world about to crash down around them, they had chosen to go out with a last, furious fling.

The present promenade and luncheon could hardly be compared to those three days in the English countryside. But something of the same mood hung about the partygoers. A significant number were in their cups, and a good many others seemed determined to get there.

"I think we should be going," Nathaniel said.

Deanna nodded her agreement. They reclaimed their mounts and with a few of the more sensible guests, began their way to the city. It was early evening when they reached there. Deanna gratefully accepted her father's suggestion that she might enjoy a hot bath in her room before dinner.

Two cheerful young maids brought the tin tub up and filled it with buckets of steaming water. As they were leaving, one of the girls lingered. With a quick glance around, she drew an envelope from her apron pocket.

"For you, miss," she said, pressing it into Deanna's hand. A quick grin of approval flashed in the maid's eyes before she was gone.

Slowly, Deanna shut the door behind her and slipped the bolt into place. Staring at the envelope, she sat down on the edge of the bed. The paper was of the finest quality, cream-colored and heavy. A red wax seal secured the flap.

Breaking the seal, she slid out a single piece of paper. Scrawled on it in black copperplate were the words: "The barn behind the stable at midnight."

Her heart was pounding as she carefully set the letter aside and began removing her clothes. Slipping into the silken water, she laid her head back against the rim of the tub, shut her eyes and began to count the hours.

Chapter Twenty-Nine

The watchman had called the hour once since Deanna had lain down fully dressed on top of the bed. Her inner sense of time told her that almost another full hour had passed. Hardly breathing, she listened to the sounds of the city beyond her window. Aside from recognizable creaks in the inn and the occasional slap of a loose shutter, she could hear nothing.

Supper was long since over and the last of the patrons departed. Her father had escorted her to her room before retiring to his own, where he was undoubtedly asleep. She, too, would have been asleep were it not for the note and the taut anticipation it provoked.

For the twelfth time, she told herself not to be a fool. She had already tempted fate once. It would be the height of folly to do so again. If she possessed any sense at all, she would meet with Nash only long enough to tell him what she had overheard Clinton say. After that, her part would be done. It would be up to him to get word to the Americans that there was a powerful traitor within their ranks.

Tell him what she'd heard, bid him good luck and depart. That was all. She would be back in her bed—and ready to sleep—before the covers had time to cool. Absolutely.

This time she would not let her emotions rule her mind. She would forget the glory of his lovemaking, the incandescent pleasure he released within her, the magnificent sense of being united with a strong, courageous man who was somehow the missing part of herself. She would forget everything except duty, reason and prudence. They would be her watchwords.

Girding for what promised to be the battle of her life with her most resourceful adversary—herself—she lost track of passing time and was startled by the watchman's call: "Mid of the night. Quiet in the town. All's well."

For him, perhaps, but her heart was beating so fast that she could scarce hear her own thoughts. Rising from the bed, she flung a dark cloak around her shoulders and cautiously eased the bar up from across the door.

Moments later, she was racing across the stable yard. The moon was high and the night clear. No one else appeared to be about as she slipped through the wide wooden door and looked around. The stable was large; there were stalls for twenty or more horses, and most of those were occupied. Drowsing mounts flicked their tails in their sleep and snorted softly. One or two, more jittery than the others, woke and eyed her briefly before nodding off again. The familiar, comforting scents of hay and straw, leather and horse, surrounded her. She moved slowly, unsure of exactly where she would go. The air inside the stable was cool. She wrapped her shawl more closely around herself and shivered.

Nash frowned. He stepped from behind the tree that had concealed him and looked toward the stable. Was that actually Deanna who had just gone in there? What would possess her to do such a thing?

He had been watching the inn since shortly after ten o'clock, waiting for a safe moment to climb the tree near Deanna's window. The plan was risky, but she'd made it clear that they needed to talk and he could think of no safer way to go about it.

Now here she was, slipping out of the inn alone and going into the stable. Surely, she wouldn't try to go riding at this time of night? Given her fondness for wandering around after dark, who knew what she might intend. He cursed under his breath and moved quickly across the stable yard.

Deanna shivered again. She was just beginning to wonder if she had somehow misunderstood Nash's note when a footfall sounded behind her. Whirling, she saw that she was no longer alone.

"There you are," she said breathlessly. "I thought perhaps I'd— Oh, never mind. There isn't time. We must speak quickly."

Nash's brows drew together. She didn't appear at all surprised to see him. Why?

He had no chance to think further. Deanna came up directly in front of him, so close that he could feel the warmth of her body. Her voice was low and tense. "You must get word to the Americans. There is a traitor in their ranks."

His eyes narrowed. Whatever he had expected, it wasn't this. Her cheeks were flushed and her eyes luminous in a most delightful way that made him want to think of almost anything other than the godawful war. Yet she seemed absolutely certain of what she was saying. He could not dismiss it. "What are you—?"

"Listen to me, it's true. I heard Clinton talking about it. There is someone the Americans believe is their agent but who is actually working for the British. Left unchecked, he will do who knows what damage."

Nash took a long breath. His mind was racing, trying to come to terms with this astounding bit of news—and with how he should respond to it. "You're saying there's a double agent?"

"Yes, of course. Washington must be told. The Americans—"

"Who is it?"

She shook her head. "I don't know. Clinton never mentioned his name or anything else that could identify him beyond the fact that the Americans believe he's working for them. The other man—whoever Clinton was talking to—seemed to think there was something shameful about all this. But the general denied it. He said the British need any edge they can get and are fortunate to have such an agent.''

''I'll bet he did,'' Nash murmured.

He was silent for a moment. A gust of wind blew through the cracks in the stable door. Deanna shivered again.

''You're cold,'' he said, and without pausing to think, drew her to him.

She was slim and pliant in his arms, her head resting on his shoulder and her heart beating with his own. He inhaled the fragrance of her hair which reminded him of a sun-washed day, and felt a sense of longing so intense that it robbed him of breath.

The stable was wrapped in quiet. There was privacy and a soft bed of hay. When would they ever have a chance to be together like this again?

She lifted her head and looked at him. No words passed between them, but the light in her eyes mirrored thoughts similar to his own. Her lips were so very close, her body so soft. He had only to...

Abruptly, he straightened and stepped away. This could not be. He had placed her at intolerable risk once by letting his passions rule him. Honor and pride, besides simple decency, demanded that he not do so again.

''We can't,'' he said, the sound of his own voice odd to his ears.

She flushed painfully and looked away.

It was all he could do not to gather her back up into his arms, throw caution to the hindmost and refuse ever to let her go again. But that choice wasn't his. For one thing, there was the startling revelation she had made. He couldn't pretend that didn't pose an enormous problem.

"Please," she said huskily, "just go. Tell the Americans..."

He nodded, glad for a reason he could not resist. "I will. Deanna—"

She shook her head, still keeping her eyes averted. "Go now, please."

Slowly, the effort tearing him apart, Nash nodded. She was right, of course, but that did nothing to ease the pain. His jaw clenched, and he turned to go. His last glimpse of her was of white lace and tumbled golden hair, stark against the shadows of the night.

Chapter Thirty

Deanna spent a largely sleepless night, kept awake by her longing for Nash. When she rose shortly after dawn, her face was pale and there were dark shadows under her eyes. She did her best to conceal both but was still not looking herself when she joined her father below for breakfast.

Nathaniel was studying a freshly printed newspaper. He looked up, saw her and began to smile, only to stop abruptly. "What's wrong?"

She shook her head quickly. "Nothing, I was just a bit restless last night. Shall we go in?" Taking his arm, she steered him toward the dining room where several guests were already seated.

Nathaniel went, but not without obvious reluctance. When they had taken their places across from each other at a table by the window, he said, "I insist you tell me. If you are feeling poorly, I will summon a physician."

Deanna winced at the thought. In her opinion, most physicians were quacks who did far more harm than good. Besides, she knew perfectly well what ailed her, and no physician could do anything about it. Perhaps one of the wise women of bygone days might have been able to manage a relief for her aching heart, but she doubted even that.

"I'm fine." She mustered a smile. "What's in the paper this morning?"

Her father hesitated, unwilling to be diverted, but finally he perused the front page and gave her a bland summary. "News from England, mainly. You'd think there was nothing going on here."

The waitress brought thick mugs of tea and a basket of bread. Nathaniel took a slice but set it on his plate untasted. "I'd like to return to Belle Haven tomorrow, if that's agreeable to you."

Deanna felt a surge of relief. More than anything, she wanted to be home. "I'd love that."

"You won't miss the city?"

"Honestly, no." Trying again to reassure him, she added, "I guess I'm just a country girl."

Her father nodded. "Perhaps it's for the best. But what about your clothes?"

"I've already arranged for them to be sent on when they're ready."

He smiled wryly. "It sounds as though you're a step ahead of me."

She reached across the table and gave his hand a quick squeeze. "As you said, it's for the best."

Nathaniel still looked unconvinced, but the waitress returned just then with the rest of their food, and he allowed himself to be diverted. He was carrying his fork to his mouth when there was a sudden disturbance by the door.

"Stand back," a loud voice ordered. "The King's business."

Several people who had been in the way immediately scurried out of it. Deanna caught a glimpse of several uniformed soldiers and at their front—Charles? What was he doing here?

Resplendent in his dress uniform, Harrow crossed the room directly toward her. Nathaniel saw him coming and smiled cordially. He began to rise in greeting. "Charles, good—"

Unsmiling, his face rigid, Harrow stared at them both. He raised a hand, cutting off Nathaniel. "Stay as you were." Curtly, he gestured to the soldiers. In an instant, they encircled the table, muskets in their hands, their eyes hard.

Ignoring the order, perhaps because he could not comprehend it, Nathaniel remained standing. His napkin dropped onto his plate. "What on earth are you doing, man?"

Charles's thin mouth parted in a cruel parody of a smile. With obvious satisfaction, he said, "Arresting your daughter, sir. You will rue the day you nurtured such a viper."

Deanna gasped. The color fled from her cheeks. Shock exploded in her. Hard on it came numbness. Suddenly, she felt like an observer set aside from the scene, watching it with astonishment.

Not so her father. He turned fiery red, rage evident in every inch of his being. "Are you mad? How dare you say such a thing? Apologize at once!"

Charles laughed. "Apologize? For catching a traitor to the Crown? I think not, old man." Harshly, he shoved Nathaniel aside and reached for Deanna.

"No," she screamed, not for her own sake but because her father was trying to intervene. Two soldiers instantly moved to stop him. They seized him harshly, holding on to him despite his great struggles.

"This is criminal," Nathaniel cried. "How can anyone do such a thing? I demand to see General Clinton at once! You won't get away with this, Harrow. I swear it!"

Charles sneered. "Swear it in hell, fool. I caught her myself, last night in the stable. She's been spying on General Clinton, trading secrets to the Americans."

An angry murmur ran round the room. Deanna struggled to breathe. Charles had a cruel hold on her. There was no possibility that she could escape. And even if she could somehow manage to, she wouldn't get far. She was trapped, without any ally except her father, and there was nothing he could do.

"Deanna?" Nathaniel said, seeing the look on her face. "What is this idiot saying?"

In misery, her eyes met his. Softly, pleading for understanding, she whispered, "I'm sorry."

Before she could say more, Charles was dragging her away. The soldiers followed. She stretched out a hand to her father, but he was already beyond her reach.

Chapter Thirty-One

The straw was damp and cold beneath her cheek. Deanna sat up, arms wrapped around herself. She was shivering convulsively, partly from the dank chill, partly from stark terror. She could not believe what had happened.

The jail was an old stone building near the river. Its inner walls were coated with slime. The sound of water splashing against the nearby piers filtered through Deanna's single barred window.

Just beyond it, people were going about their daily business. Shops were opening, ships arriving and leaving, soldiers drilling, women marketing, men at work and children at their lessons. All so blessedly ordinary.

Her throat tightened. Panic swelled within her. Valiantly, she fought it down but not before wondering how much longer her courage could last.

She had been alone for several hours, ever since Charles pushed her into the cell and slammed the door behind her. Already, the passage of time was becom-

ing uncertain. She couldn't tell for sure if it was mid-
or late morning. All she really knew was that her father must be desperately worried. Thoughts of what he
must be enduring stabbed through her. She sat down
on the straw and buried her face in her hands.

The door creaked. She looked up with a spurt of
hope, only to have it die when she saw the man standing outside. Charles.

He seemed insufferably pleased with himself. Smiling, he stepped into the cell and shut the door behind
him. His eyes ran over her, lingering on her breasts
and hips. "Enjoying yourself, my dear?"

Deanna got to her feet. The cell was so small that
there was nowhere for her to go, but she felt safer
standing.

"Where is my father?"

His eyebrows rose. "Your father? How should I
know? Perhaps he's left town."

"He wouldn't do that. He would stay to help me."

"Are you sure? I saw the look on his face when you
admitted what you had done. He appeared as thoroughly disgusted with you as any right-thinking person would be." Charles took a step closer, his smile
deepening. "Incidentally, that admission will be
damning against you in court."

"C-court?"

"Of course, court. What did you think, that we'd
hang you without a trial? That would hardly be civilized, would it?"

Bile rose in Deanna's throat. She took a deep
breath, praying for calm. "You have no real evidence

against me. It's only your word against mine for what was said in the stable. Besides, you will have to account for your own presence there.''

He scowled, angered by her courage. "I will say that I brought a sick horse for care and went to check on it.''

"At midnight? Who will believe that? Wouldn't any horse have received better care at the regimental stable?''

"Not necessarily. The innkeeper is known for his skill with animals.''

Deanna had no idea if that was true or not. Charles was ruthless and arrogant, but that didn't prevent him from being clever. "Even so, the idea of you leaving your bed to check on an ill horse won't stretch very far.''

He bent down slightly so that they were eye to eye. With rage evident in every word, he said, "No one will care, you little fool. No one will think twice about why *I* was in the stable. All they'll care about is you.''

"And Nash. What about him? If you are such a valiant protector of Mother England, why didn't you prevent him from getting away?''

Charles rocked back slightly on his heels as though she had struck him. His eyes glittered dangerously. "An odd question about a man you are obviously fond of.''

She refused to be baited. He had seen what he had seen. She could hardly try to convince him that her feelings for Nash were neutral. But she didn't have to discuss them, either.

"That is neither here nor there. No court will think well of you for letting him go." Scathingly, she added, "Not that it's any mystery why you would. You were frightened, plain and simple."

Barely were the words out than she regretted them. Anger and pain were all very well, but she would have been wise to hold on to just a little caution. Now it was too late.

Charles's hand lashed out, catching her full across the face. She cried out and fell backward but managed to regain her balance. He was advancing on her, his fists clenched.

"Get away from me!"

"Not until I've taught you a much-needed lesson, bitch. How dare you betray me? How dare you seek another man? You belong to me. You have ever since England. I'll teach you—"

He raised his hand again. Deanna bent over, trying to shield herself from the blow. It caught her across the shoulders, knocking the wind from her. Her knees weakened, and again she thought she would fall.

Pride came to her rescue. She would not allow Charles, or any other man, to do this to her. Whatever the cost, she would fight back. Desperately, she looked around for some kind of weapon, but there was nothing in sight. She had only the simple dress she had donned that morning...that and the long pins she had used to put up her hair when she woke too tired to brush it fully.

Swiftly, she yanked one of the pins out and turned to face Charles. "Get away from me."

Seeing what she held, he laughed. "You need to be shown what a real dagger looks like. Apparently, Nash wasn't the man for the job."

Sickness roiled in her but she refused to let him see it. "Get back, I mean it."

"And I mean this," he said as he reached for her.

Deanna didn't hesitate. No weakening of will, no hidden timidity seized her. She knew that what she was doing was absolutely right and she did it well.

The pin raked down Charles' cheek, drawing blood. He yelled and clamped his hand to the wound. "Bitch!"

"Your vocabulary grows as tiresome as your presence. Go bother someone else."

"I...I..." Shaking in fury, he advanced on her.

"Be careful," she warned. "Your case against me won't hold up. If you testify in court the way you say, you'll be labeled a coward for letting Nash go. Or even worse, suspected of being a traitor yourself."

Charles's eyes narrowed. A look of pure cunning flickered across his face. "Will I? You're as stupid as you are rebellious. Who do you think Clinton was talking about?"

"What do you mean?"

"That Nash is the traitor, you fool. It's really rather funny when you think about it. You warned him about himself."

"No!" It couldn't be true. Nash had risked his life to come to Belle Haven to spy on Clinton. He had killed two British soldiers in the process. Or had he?

She had only his word that he'd fought with the two and only his explanation of what he was doing there.

No, she wouldn't think like that. He was courageous and daring, fighting for what he believed sacred. Charles was a cruel, angry man. He would anything.

"Think," he snarled. "Nash and I were at school together. He grew up as one of us. Do you really think he changed his views when he came back here? Do you honestly think he believes all this nonsense about freedom and equality? For God's sake, how foolish can you be?"

Deanna shook her head. "You're lying."

"Who lured you to the stable? Who sent the note that trapped you? We were in it together, he and I. He'll testify against you himself."

"I don't believe you. I don't!"

"Believe what you want. You were hoodwinked by the best, I'll say that. And I hope you at least enjoyed it, because you're going to pay a hell of a price."

More than even he knew. Deep inside, a part of herself that had grown and flowered since Nash's touch suddenly went still. Slowly, irresistibly, it began to shrivel.

"It's a shame in a way," Charles said more calmly. "I would have treated you very well. But as it is—" He broke off and reached for her again. "I would hate to see you hang without having had you first."

His mouth twisted. An unholy light burned in his eyes. "Nash said you were good. Let's see if he was right."

A sob of revulsion broke from Deanna. The pin was still in her hand; she had to use it. But the terrible anguish was growing inside her, robbing her of strength. Charles's arms were around her, his hand pulling her head back, his mouth almost on hers. Her will had vanished. She felt as though she was dead inside.

The cell door opened. A young officer stood just outside in the corridor. He looked from Deanna to Charles, plainly shocked by what he saw. "Sir?"

"What in bloody hell do you want?" Charles demanded.

"General Clinton wishes to see you." For good measure, he added, "Immediately."

Charles cursed under his breath but not even he could gainsay the general. With a hard shove, he pushed Deanna down onto the straw. Straightening his stock, he said, "I'll be back, sweetling. Count on it."

The younger man jumped out of his way as Charles stormed past. He glanced sympathetically at Deanna.

Before she could move or speak, the door slammed shut again with a ring of finality.

Chapter Thirty-Two

"I must see the general. It is of the utmost urgency."

The aide nodded, his eyes never leaving Nathaniel's face. Quietly, he said, "I understand, Mr. Marlowe. However, General Clinton is not available at the moment."

Nathaniel took a deep breath, struggling for calm. Ever since the extraordinary scene in the inn, he had been fighting a growing sense of unreality. The world had taken on the guise of a nightmare, one he could not seem to wake from. "He has to be available. My daughter has been wrongly arrested and taken to jail. She is an innocent young woman. It is unthinkable that she should be left in such a place."

The aide sighed. He rose from behind the inlaid desk that was his station and walked round to the front. "I am sorry but there is nothing I can do."

"There has to be! She—"

The aide laid a hand on Nathaniel's arm. With the other, he gestured to the two guards posted nearby.

"Miss Marlowe was detained on a writ signed by the general himself. He believed there was sufficient cause to bind her over pending investigation."

"That's insane! She's my daughter. She would never—"

"I'm sorry," the aide said. He nodded to the guards. "You will have to leave now, sir."

Nathaniel protested. But nothing he said or did was to any avail. In short order, he was out on the street and the door to the general's residence shut against him.

"Can't do it," the warden said. He was a fat, greasy man with a black-toothed smile and an air of self-importance. "Orders from the general hisself. No visitors."

"You are holding my daughter," Nathaniel said. "She has been falsely accused. Surely, it will do no harm to allow me to speak with her for a few minutes." He reached into his pocket and withdrew his coin purse.

The warden looked at it with unconcealed interest. Reluctantly, he shook his head. "Orders are orders. Stretch 'em too far and they'll slap right back at you, sure as not." In what was apparently a concession for him, he added, "Sorry."

Nathaniel tried again, going so far as to dangle the money. But he could not convince the man, and after a time he went away. Slowly, he walked around the corner of the jail. Although he had strolled by it many times while in New York, he had never really looked at it before.

It was a hideous building, low and squat with nothing to recommend it whatsoever. Worse yet—if the barred windows were anything to go by—the cells were located close to the waterline. They would be cold and dank even on a fair day.

Pausing, he glanced over his shoulder to be sure he was unobserved. As softly as he could manage, he called, "Deanna?"

There was no answer, only a faint cough from the other side. Moving on, he stopped beneath the next window and tried again. Once more, there was no result.

Nathaniel persisted. Somehow, he had to reach her, if only to offer the comfort of a few words. Twice more he tried, a third time, a fourth. Finally, on the seventh try, his efforts were rewarded.

"Deanna?"

"Father?"

"Thank the Lord I've found you."

"Oh, Father, I'm so sorry. I can't begin to tell you." Her voice sounded weak and tremulous, not at all like his brave Deanna. Grief surged in him. No matter what she had done, she was his child. He would protect her to his dying breath. "Never mind, I've only got a few moments. Clinton's refused to see me but I'll find some way to get help. I swear it."

"There is no way," Deanna said softly. "I was betrayed." Her voice caught.

No response came.

"Father?"

"I'm still here." Tears stung his eyes. He could not believe that her cause was hopeless.

"Don't hate me."

"Hate you? As though I could ever do such a thing. I love you."

"Then do this for me. Go home to Belle Haven. Find Fletcher Wesskum. Tell him to come quickly. I must speak with him before..."

"Before what?"

"Nothing, only do it. I beseech you."

"What is Wesskum to you?"

In fact, Deanna barely knew the man. But Nash had said he would know his whereabouts. She had to pray that didn't mean Wesskum was also in league with the British. If she was wrong about that, she was truly lost. "Only tell him, please."

A wagon was coming around the side of the jail, full of slops to be dumped in the river. Nathaniel turned away from the wall. His back to it, hands clenched, he said, "All right."

He heard a soft sigh of relief, nothing more, as he moved quickly away, but it was enough to sustain him as he hurried to find the swiftest boat to carry him home.

The wind was fair and the water calm. Nathaniel reached Belle Haven as night was settling over the land. He asked in the tavern for Wesskum but was told no one had seen him in several days. With darkness descending, he would have to turn for home, but not without first leaving word that he needed to see the woodsman as soon as possible.

Martha met him at the door. Without preamble, the old woman demanded, "Why are you home so soon, and where's my lass?"

Nathaniel loathed the very idea of telling her, but he had known Martha far too long to think she could be deceived.

"Sit down." As gently as he could, he told her.

She was white and trembling when he finished. In seconds, however, she was on her feet.

"Where are you going?" he asked.

"To get Lucas. He has to know."

"I don't see what he's going to be able to do."

She turned, hands on her hips, and glared at him. "Well, for one thing, Nathaniel Marlowe, he can go help you look for Fletcher Wesskum. We are going to find that man before the sun is up or I am damn well going to go after her myself."

Nathaniel stared, amazed by her temerity. But after a moment, he laughed. For the first time since leaving New York, he found a spurt of hope. "Damned if you aren't right, Martha. You go get him. I'll saddle up the horses."

"Saddle three."

"Three? You can't be serious."

"Damn straight I am. She's my baby girl, same as if I'd borne her, and no one—I mean no one—is going to do her harm. Now git!"

Nathaniel got. He had one horse saddled and bridled and was starting on the second when Lucas joined him.

Lucas said little, only nodded and gestured toward the wood. "I know some of the places Fletcher likes to camp. Martha knows some others. But just in case he's picked tonight to go fishing, how about you track along the river?"

"He fishes at night?" Nathaniel asked.

Lucas grinned. "He does anything he pleases, day or night."

"I still don't see how he can help my girl."

"He won't unless we can find him," Martha said as she joined them. Lucas gave her a boost into the saddle. She was the first to ride out, leaving the men to follow quickly.

Chapter Thirty-Three

"Eight...nine...ten..." Deanna counted softly as she paced back and forth across the narrow cell. It was twelve paces from wall to wall, ten from the window to the door. She had walked it over and over, sometimes in a cross, sometimes a star or rectangle, alternating the patterns, forcing herself to concentrate.

The dimensions of the room were real. If she focused on them long enough, she could keep her mind from whirling away into a chasm of fear and dread. Or so she hoped.

Ten days had passed since Charles's sudden appearance at the inn. She had marked each day on the wall near the window using a chip of stone. Five days were passed since his last appearance outside the cell door.

General Clinton had ordered that she be held incommunicado. No one could see her, not even her father or the attorney he had engaged upon his return from Belle Haven.

Charles had managed to get the rules bent, but not entirely broken. He had been allowed no further than the corridor outside her locked door. She supposed she ought to be grateful, but he had used each occasion to taunt her, reminding her of what a fool she had been to trust Nash.

The words had fallen like acid on her soul. Even when he no longer came—five days now—she could still hear his words.

The warden, who brought the food her father had procured, had unbent enough to tell her that the general was out of town and that he had taken Charles with him. Her trial would not begin until they returned, probably within a few days.

So her reprieve, such as it was, would be short-lived.

She stopped walking and pressed her hands against the wall. Her hair was uncombed and matted, her dress filthy. With each passing day, she was able to eat less and less.

The crack of sunlight that shone through the single window tormented her. Sometimes she imagined she saw it at night, beckoning in her nightmare-torn sleep. It seemed to be receding farther and farther away, leaving her in a darkness as deep as the grave.

Why hadn't Fletcher Wesskum come? Her father had gotten word to her that he'd found the woodsman and told him what had happened. Wesskum had promised to help. Still, there was no sign of him. Where had he gone?

A sob broke from her. She pressed her lips together fiercely. Tears slid down her wan cheeks. Earlier on, she had made it a point not to cry. But that strength was beyond her now. Wearily, she leaned her head against the wall and let the tears come.

Slowly, the sun passed beyond reach of the window. Twilight descended, and hard upon it darkness. Night wrapped round the jail, smothering hope.

Nash paused immediately inside the door to let his eyes adjust to the dim light. The air was chill and dank, smelling of straw, unwashed bodies and despair. He flicked a stray speck of dust from the midnight blue cloak he wore over meticulously tailored buff breeches, a high-collared silk shirt and a black velvet waistcoat.

A heavy gold insignia ring gleamed on his left hand. He was cleanly shaven, and his skin was burnished by the sun. Powerfully muscled, graceful in his every movement, he was clearly a man of wealth and power. Exactly as he needed to be perceived on this night when so much depended on what happened in the next few minutes.

A young, rawboned man stood near the door. He wore the uniform of a British regular but his breeches were dirty, his boots unpolished and he needed to shave.

"Yer late," he said.

"Am I? And who might you be?"

"Regis Fuller, that's who. The warden's gone for his supper. He said you were coming." His lips split in a leer. "For the woman, isn't it? The rebel bitch Harrow caught. Pretty piece, she is, but I'll wager you already know that.''

Nash considered his alternatives. Tempted though he was to punish the man for his insolence, that would take time, something he had very little of. Turning toward an iron-bound door at the back of room, he said, ''Miss Marlowe is ready, is she not?''

''I don't know if she is or not,'' the man said, scurrying after him. ''All I know is she's supposed to go with you.'' He grinned. ''Good luck to you, guv. Yer going to need it.''

The door gave way, opening to a long corridor with cells on either side. ''Show me,'' Nash said.

At the far end, the man stopped and pointed. ''She's in there.''

''Open it.''

Hinges creaked. Nash cursed under his breath. He seized the lantern suspended from a hook on the wall and stepped into the cell.

The circle of light illuminated a small space. Dirty straw was piled in one corner. Something moved in it.

''Deanna?''

A faint moan reached him. He cursed and went quickly toward the sound. Bending down, he reached out a hand.

She recoiled instantly. ''Get away from me or I'll kill you.''

His arm lashed out, closing hard around her waist. He lifted her effortlessly.

"Let me go." She curled her hand into a fist, attempting to strike him.

"Ye've got to sign for her," the man remembered. "Warden said you must."

Ignoring Deanna's continued struggles, Nash seized the stump of charcoal and scrawled his name.

"Where're you going?" the man asked as Nash walked swiftly out of the jail, carrying Deanna.

Nash ignored him. A carriage was waiting directly in front. Nash thrust the door opened and pushed Deanna inside, following her quickly. She lashed out suddenly, kicking him in the shin. The blow caught him unawares.

"Stop that," he ordered as the carriage began to move.

Instead, she struck out again, landing a blow on his jaw. He cursed and took hold of her. She felt so fragile in his arms and so weak. Rage tore at him again. More harshly than he intended, he said, "Deanna, stop this. It's me, Nash."

She seemed not to hear him. Her struggles redoubled. Desperate to avoid hurting her, and at a loss to understand why she was acting like this, he was unprepared when she suddenly wrenched her knee up and drove it into his chest. The blow drove the air from him, and for a scant instant caused his grip to lessen.

Deanna tore herself from his grasp and thrust the carriage door open. Cool, evening air poured in. The horses' hooves clattered over cobblestones slick from an earlier rain shower.

The realization of what she meant to do struck Nash like a thunder clap. He reached out, his fingers brushing her waist. *"Deanna, no!"*

Chapter Thirty-Four

A second later, an inch more and he would have lost her. The realization ran like ice through Nash even as he pulled Deanna back into the carriage. She was still struggling, but her efforts were becoming weaker.

Clasping her to him with one arm, he yanked the carriage door closed and fell back against the seat. His breath was ragged and his heart threatened to explode. How could she have done such a thing? Why would she? Had the days in jail so deranged her mind that she was truly mad? Above all, what in God's name was he to do?

Fiercely, he held her to him. She whimpered as the last of her strength left her and she went limp.

"Need any help?" the driver asked.

Nash shook his head. He lifted Deanna carefully from the carriage. They were well out of the city, having followed the road that ran north to Greenwich Village. Just beyond it was a small landing where boats put in.

"Head on back," Nash said. "Get rid of the carriage and make yourself scarce. If anyone asks, you never saw me tonight."

The man nodded. He was well paid and loyal besides.

There would be no problem with him, Nash thought as he walked swiftly toward the landing. The weather had turned colder and although he had wrapped Deanna in his cloak, he was still concerned she would become chilled.

A torch flared near the landing. Fletcher Wesskum was waiting. He glanced from Nash to the woman asleep in his arms. "Everyone all right?"

"Fine, so far," Nash said. "Let's go."

Fletcher led the way to the boat tied to the landing. He doused the torch in the water, but not before lighting the small lantern hanging in the prow. The oars were muffled. They made barely a sound as the village slipped away behind them.

"Calm tonight," Fletcher said.

Nash nodded. They had a long way to go. He found a blanket and wrapped it, too, around Deanna. She stirred but did not wake.

They headed south toward the tip of Manhattan Island. Their course required them to pass some of the most heavily manned British positions. But there was no alternative since the nearest safety lay to the south.

A half hour later, they saw the lights of a British yawl lying offshore. Fletcher muffled the lantern. With the oars barely touching water, they glided past.

A little farther on, the silhouette of cannons emerging from a stone bunker could be seen. The coast was extensively fortified. They could expect to see many more of the same fortifications before finally emerging on the other side of the island, near the mouth of the Hudson River.

The current strengthened. Fletcher had to pull hard to keep them on course. His efforts were rewarded when a short time later they saw a faint glimmer of light along the New Jersey shore.

"They're waiting," Nash said.

"Told you they would be."

The Indians came out of the night, moving silently. They helped secure the boat and stood by while Nash lifted Deanna from it.

"Thank you," Nash said, turning to Fletcher.

The woodsman nodded. He flashed a grin. "She's gonna be kinda surprised when she wakes up."

"I'll be glad if that's all she is," Nash said, remembering Deanna's actions in the carriage. He would think about that later; the Indians were waiting. He gave a final nod to Wesskum and followed them.

A narrow path led from the water's edge deep into the surrounding forest. It was covered with pine needles which absorbed every sound. In a small clearing about a quarter mile from the river, a log house stood.

One of the Indians led the way inside. He lit a small fire in a stone pit dug in the ground. When Nash had lowered Deanna onto a bed of hides, the Indian handed him a musket.

"Wesskum claims you're a good shot."

Nash hoisted the weapon, finding it well balanced. He was glad to have it, but he was also honest. "I prefer a knife."

The man smiled his approval. "Over there," he said, indicating a pile on the floor. "Also food, clothes and some medicines for the woman, in case she needs them."

Nash's face was grim. "She may very well. She was badly treated."

"This whole thing is ending badly, but at least it is ending."

"Is it? I've been out of touch for several days."

The Indian nodded. "Cornwallis is retreating to Yorktown. Word is he intends to make his stand there."

It wasn't a bad choice. The site was easily defensible, provided Cornwallis had enough men to do it with. Did he?

Nash pushed the thought aside and said farewell, offering his thanks, as well.

With the Indians' departure, he turned his full attention to Deanna. She lay on her side, her face turned away from him. As he knelt beside her, he noticed a bruise on her cheek, several days old by the look of it.

Cursing, he eased the blanket from around her and unwound his cloak. By the light of the small fire, the damage of ten days' confinement could be clearly seen. Her hair was matted with dust and grime, her face streaked with dirt. The bodice of her gown was torn, revealing purpling bruises on her shoulders. The dress, which he remembered as fitting her perfectly, now hung loosely. Looking farther, he found marks on her palms where she had dug her nails into them.

His mouth set in a hard line. Leaving her briefly, he went outside to find water. He returned with a bucketful and set it over the fire. Then he removed his frock coat. With his sleeves rolled up, he returned to Deanna.

She was so exhausted that she showed no sign of waking even as he carefully turned her over and undid the buttons down the back of her dress. The fire, small as it was, gave off enough heat to warm the log house—and Deanna—comfortably. Slowly, he slipped the dress from her. Beneath it, she wore a white camisole and petticoat. Fortunately, she hadn't bothered with stays, but then she was slender enough to have no need of them.

Struggling to keep his mind on the task at hand, Nash removed her shoes and rolled down the thin cotton stockings secured by garters. That done, he took a manful breath and slipped the camisole over her head. The petticoat followed.

When she lay naked on the bed of hides, he sat back and allowed himself the luxury of looking at her. But only for a moment. The bluish shadows along her ribs and the deep hollows on either side of her hips spoke forcibly of her suffering. She was still an exquisitely beautiful woman, easily the loveliest he had ever seen. But she was also in dire need of care.

With a soft cotton cloth dipped in the heated water, he gently began to wash the grime from her body. She stirred a little but remained deeply asleep. His breath caught as he passed the cloth over her breasts. Her nipples puckered, becoming hard beneath his touch. She made a small sound of contentment.

Telling himself that only the world's worst churl would be tempted to take advantage of a woman's unconscious response, he finished bathing her quickly. The camisole and petticoat she had worn were filthy; he couldn't possibly put them on her. But there were several clean blankets in the pack. These he laid over her. She sighed and snuggled farther into the hides.

Next, he set about to wash her hair. For a brief moment he hesitated, not wanting to wake her. But her hair was filthy, and he knew she would be more comfortable to have it clean. Using a brush, he got out the worst of the tangles, then fetched fresh warm water. Going slowly, so as not to wet the blankets, he carefully washed strand after strand. Gradually, the dirt and dust vanished, revealing the red-gold glory hidden beneath.

When he was finished, he looked around for something to dry it with. His shirt was clean, he'd only worn it a few hours. Stripping it off, he gently squeezed the water out until only a slight dampness remained. When he brushed her hair again, it lay in a shining mass spread out over the hides.

Satisfied, he went outside to empty the bucket, returning to find Deanna still fast asleep. She lay on her side, one hand drawn up so that her fingers curled beneath her chin. With her features relaxed and her defiant green eyes closed, she looked achingly vulnerable.

Also, exquisitely tempting. Ignoring the sudden hardening of his body, he added wood to the fire, then went through the supplies the Indians had left. Assured that he had everything they needed, he secured the pack. As he did, fatigue washed over him.

When had he last slept? Three days ago, before Wesskum found him? That sounded about right. Except for a few naps snatched on the back of a horse or in the prow of a boat, he had been awake continuously.

But Deanna was safe now and cared for. The release of tension forced him to confront the exhaustion he had managed to hold at bay. The bed of hides suddenly looked tempting. He hesitated, but the only alternative was the hard ground.

Telling himself there was no harm in merely holding her, he lay down beside Deanna and drew her into his arms. Moments later, he, too, slept.

Chapter Thirty-Five

Deanna was dreaming. In her dream, she was running across a field washed by sunshine. Birds were singing, the sun was shining and she felt blissfully free. Far in the back of her mind, she felt surprised. Of late, sleep had meant nightmares. But this was entirely different. She couldn't remember ever feeling so completely happy.

Well, yes, actually she could. The memory warmed her cheeks. But it didn't matter. This was only a dream. Nothing could hurt her. She could think of Nash safely.

Or could she? Her brow furrowed. There was something about Nash, something cold and terrible. The bright dream twisted, the sun faded. She was suddenly very afraid.

Deep in the sleep of exhaustion, Nash nonetheless felt the change in Deanna. Slowly, a part of him resisting, he drove upward to consciousness. "What...?" he murmured groggily.

The fire had almost died, but the gray light of pre-dawn was seeping through the walls of the log house. He could make out her face.

She was frightened. Still half-asleep, hardly aware of what he was doing, he threw back the covers that had chastely separated them all night and gathered her close against him. Her bare breasts nestled against his chest. The warmth of her skin drove out the mild chill of his own. Fire leapt in his loins as his body responded instantly.

His mind followed more slowly. She was under him on the hide bed, his hands tangled in her hair, before he fully realized what he was doing.

Driven though he was, engulfed in hot, surging desire, he hesitated. Muscle-corded arms held his weight off her. He was suddenly acutely aware of her vulnerability and of how very easy it would be to exploit that.

The thought of doing that filled him with disgust. She had been through far too much. What she needed most was care and rest, not the passion that seemed to have taken possession of his very soul.

He looked into her face, no longer pale, and saw with a start that her eyes were open. The forest-green depths were unfathomable. They glittered with shards of gold that seemed torn from the sun or from some deep, hidden treasure trove never meant for the light of day. "Deanna?"

Her lips parted on a breath of sound. His name? He couldn't be sure. But there was little doubt of what the sudden touch of her breasts against his chest meant.

Raising herself slightly, she twined her arms around his neck in a gesture both natural and provocative.

Nash groaned as wave after wave of desire crashed through him. Before such a battering, his good intentions wavered. He was, after all, only human.

Still, he tried. The muscles of his arms corded as he lifted himself from her. Her embrace tightened. She made a soft sound in her throat as she drew him back to her.

This was better. The sunshine had returned and with it the feeling of unbridled freedom. Whatever that cold, terrible thing was, it had gone away. Best yet, Nash was here, strong, passionate, wonderful.

The terrifying experiences of recent days slipped from her as though they had never been. Only the smallest shadow of memory remained, but it was enough to make her hold on fiercely to the man who was at once her lover and protector.

Instincts as ancient as womanhood stirred within her. Her hips raised slightly, the apex of her thighs brushing against him. Slowly, she frowned. This wasn't right.

Her hand drifted down, encountering the waistband of his breeches. He said something harsh and rasping, but caught as she was between exhaustion and passion, the words had no meaning. Nothing did, except the overwhelming need to be as close to him as possible. Moaning softly, she cupped the bulge of his manhood in her palm and squeezed lightly.

Nash gritted his teeth to keep from crying out. Her artless innocence was more enticing than the skills of the most practiced courtesan. He didn't understand how that could be, but neither could he deny it. With a single touch, she mocked his tenuous self-control. With a brush of her nipples against his chest, she shattered what little was left of it.

He moved abruptly, stripping off his breeches and kicking them away. Naked, he came to her, gathering her into his arms. His big hands stroked down her back to cup her buttocks. Kneading them lightly, he slipped his thumbs into the soft, moist folds between her thighs.

Deanna cried out. The sun was burning, the day incandescent. She trembled convulsively and clung to him. His mouth lowered, seizing first one nipple, then the other. He sucked hard, raking the aching tips with his teeth, tonguing them, his roughened jaw scraping over her delicate skin.

Her legs fell open. Together, they tumbled back across the bed of hides. All thought, all restraint had been stripped from Nash. Still, enough of a remnant of reason remained that he did not immediately lay her beneath him and plunge his length deep within.

Holding her by the hips, he trailed hot kisses across her dimpled navel and satiny abdomen. His fingers found her again, teasing, arousing, until she sobbed his name and tried desperately to draw him to her.

She cried out again in mingled shock and delight when his mouth replaced his fingers. Driving her higher and higher, he waited until the first tremors began to quake through her. Only then did he part her legs yet farther and slowly, groaning with the exquisite pleasure of it, sink himself into her.

She was hot and wet, but so tight that he feared he might hurt her. Yet when he made to withdraw, she arched her back, her hands sliding down his to clasp his sinewy hips and hold him to her.

Sweet spasms of approaching release contracted around him. He shut his eyes against the force of almost unbearable pleasure. The last shred of hesitation vanished as though it had never been.

He thrust again, harder and deeper, over and over, half lifting her off the bed in the fury of his need. Until at last the world shattered around them both and he collapsed, drained, on top of her.

Chapter Thirty-Six

Deanna woke to a sense of well-being greater than any she had ever known. She stretched languorously, raising her arms above her head and wiggling her toes into the warm, soft bottom of the bed where she—

Bed? Her eyes opened wide. Instantly, they shut again as sunlight, ten days all but unseen, stung them. The cell, the clump of filthy straw, the dank smell of the river, were gone. In their place were comfort and radiant day.

Abruptly, she remembered Nash, the carriage, her struggle. The dream. She paled and sat up, only to discover that she was naked. Gasping, she dragged a blanket around herself and got to her feet shakily.

Wherever she was, the ceiling was so low that her head almost brushed it. Not only that, there was no furniture. Except for the bed of hides, a leather pack and a stone fire pit, the structure was empty. The walls were of wooden logs chinked with mud. But the mud had eroded, probably since the winter, leaving nu-

merous openings. Through them sunlight streamed.
And through them, too, Deanna peeked.

She was in a clearing surrounded by forest. Two
horses were tethered nearby. A cook fire was going,
and by it, drinking from a tin cup, stood ... *Nash*.

She turned cold. It hadn't been a dream. It was real.
The lingering echoes of pleasure still resonated within
her. She had made love with him—despite everything
she knew, despite all the betrayal, despite dignity and
pride, she had given herself to this man. Again.

She bit down hard on her clenched fist to keep from
screaming. How could she have so betrayed herself?
What treacherous part of her nature had led her to
behave in such a way?

Desperately, she looked around for her clothes but
they were nowhere to be seen. Her gaze fell on the
pack. Opening it, she breathed a sigh of relief.

Inside were down-soft breeches small enough to fit
her, a linen shirt, a boy's frock coat and even a felt
hat. The garments were exceedingly strange but at least
they would cover her. Quickly, she dressed, tucking
her hair up.

Moving toward the door, she paused, struck by the
unexpected freedom of walking without the confines
of a long skirt. No wonder men were able to get about
so much more agilely. It wasn't nature that made them
so. It was simply fashion.

Cautiously, she stepped outside. Nash had his back
to her. With just a little luck, she could slip away into
the surrounding woods and be gone before he knew it.

What she would do after that she couldn't begin to think of. All that mattered was getting away.

But this was not Belle Haven where she could move with impunity, knowing every rise and fall of the land as perfectly as she did the contours of her own face. This was unknown territory.

A branch snapped beneath her foot. She froze.

"Damn." The gruffly voiced expletive was followed instantly by steps crunching swiftly over the ground toward her.

Deanna's momentary paralysis vanished. Unencumbered by the usual heavy skirts, she ran as swiftly as a doe, leaping over a fallen log to vanish among the trees.

Nash cursed again. He'd left her asleep in the log house, convinced that she would remain that way for some time and glad of a chance to deal with his own feelings in private. That had been a mistake. He was no closer to sorting out his confusing tumult of thoughts, and he had lost Deanna, if only temporarily.

She was quick, he gave her that, and daring. But when it came to moving through a forest undetected, she was an utter novice.

He was not. What boyhood in England had not prepared him for, manhood in war had. He'd gone out of his way to learn as much as he could about survival in the thick primal forests that covered most of the land.

Wesskum had taught him some, as had other woodsmen. He wasn't as good as they were, not yet, at least. But faced with the challenge of tracking Deanna, he was more than good enough.

He could hear her crashing through the underbrush directly ahead. Grimly, he smiled. For a slender woman, she managed to make an unholy amount of noise.

In the grip of panic, Deanna hardly knew what she was doing. She had no idea in what direction she was heading. The forest had thickened around her, becoming so dense that she was hard pressed to get through it. Wild grasses tall as her waist slowed her at every step. Vines twining over the ground tripped her. Brambles pulled at her clothes and caught her skin.

Scratched and bleeding, bruised by several falls and almost out of breath, she kept going. Just ahead, she caught a glimpse of water—a river—and she renewed her efforts. She was a good swimmer. If she could reach the river, she might have a real chance of escape.

The trees thinned at the river's edge. She broke free of the underbrush and ran forward. In just another moment, she would be—

A steely arm wrapped around her waist, pulling her back. Her feet left the ground. She kicked out with arms and legs alike, but it was useless. Easily evading her blows, Nash carried her up the riverbank.

"Fool," he said as he set her down but kept a hard hand on her arm. "Just what did you think you were doing?"

Deanna's breathing was ragged, her heart beating fiercely, and not all because of her exertions. "Trying to get away from you."

"Why?"

When she did not reply, or even look at him, he caught hold of her chin and angrily turned her to face him. "Look at me."

She did, but only a quick glance out of the corner of her eye. It was enough to remind her of every incandescent moment of the night before. Fiercely, she blushed. "Let me go."

His self-control—never reliable where she was concerned—threatened to crumble yet again. Grimly summoning patience, he tightened his hold on her. "I didn't go to all this trouble so you could walk right back into a British jail. The least you owe me is an explanation. What the hell is wrong with you?"

Deanna's eyes flashed dangerously.

Being a prudent man, Nash stepped back a notch. He knew her well enough to realize that her temper was at least a match for his own.

"Wrong?" she echoed. "With me? Nothing at all except being the world's worst fool." Her voice caught. She turned her head away, but not before he saw the sudden sheen of tears in her eyes.

Astonishment roared through him. What could possibly have happened to bring this proud woman to the point of tears? Had her treatment in jail been worse than he'd realized? Or was it their lovemaking she so bitterly regretted?

This last possibility made him wince. Granted, his behavior had been reprehensible. But if she had resisted even in the least, if she'd merely said no, he would have stopped instantly. On that point, he was absolutely sure. Quietly, dreading what he would hear, he asked, "What are you talking about?"

A tremor ran through her. "I blame myself."

He was going to be patient, even if it killed him. "For what?"

"Trusting you."

There it was, stark and ugly, the accusation he had most feared. He took a breath against the pain and wished for just a moment that he was in a battle he knew how to win.

"I'm sorry."

She looked at him in astonishment. "Sorry? You're sorry? Is that supposed to mean something?"

He had moved through drawing rooms where intrigue was the breath of life, dealt with courtiers and courtesans, fought in duels and in war, made a fortune and begun the making of a nation. But never had he felt at such a loss as he did at this moment, confronted with this woman. "It means I'm sorry, I regret what happened."

"So do I," she said, trying to wrench her arm away.

But he had learned to know her at least well enough to anticipate that she would never give up so easily. He kept his hold and tried to speak soothingly. "I was exhausted last night. We both were. I don't think either of us fully realized what was happening until it was too late."

Her cheeks burned. Fiercely, she said, "If you have an ounce of decency, you will not speak of that again."

All right, she didn't want to talk about their lovemaking. But if they couldn't talk about it, how could he convince her that he truly hadn't meant to take advantage of her? She seemed to have no memory of her own eager participation, and it would be the height of churlishness to remind her.

Stymied, he was utterly unprepared when she said, "You know perfectly well it has nothing to do with anything."

Chapter Thirty-Seven

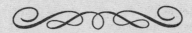

He was hurt. It was an absurd reaction but there it was. Perhaps it was vanity, but he really would have preferred to think that their lovemaking had some significance—however slight—for Deanna.

Apparently not. Her dismissal of it with a handful of words left him at first stunned, then angry. She was a gently reared woman—never mind that her father had afforded her a shocking amount of liberty. She should have been reeling from what they'd done. Instead, she appeared to take it as casually as a man might a night beneath the covers with a light skirt. Only this time, the skirt—so to speak—was on him. He found the sensation singularly unpleasant.

"I see," he said, not because he did but because he had to say something. She couldn't have it all her way. "In that case, would you mind telling me why you're leaving so hastily?"

"To get away from you."

Whoever had said women were chatterboxes hadn't

met Deanna. Bending over so that they were on eye level, he stared hard at her. "Why?"

"You know why."

That did it. She had toyed with his emotions, insulted his manhood and left him floundering. Now she had the nerve to claim he should understand. "No, I don't," he almost shouted.

She looked at him with scorn. As though delivering a death blow, she said, "Charles told me."

Charles. He was at the root of all this, curse his blighted hide. If Nash ever got his hands on the Englishman again, he would... "Told you what? And don't," he added quickly, "tell me I know what. I do not know. I want you to tell me. In fact, I damn well insist on it."

She glared, her eyes shooting daggers, but the slight trembling of her mouth suggested there was real pain beneath the anger. So quietly that Nash could hardly hear, she said, "He told me that you're the traitor."

Through the fog of shock that immediately enveloped him, one thought stood out clearly. "You believe him."

"How can I not? The two of you were in league together." When he would have denied it, she charged, "You sent the note that drew me to the stable. Charles was waiting to hear what I'd be fool enough to say and carry it back to Clinton." Her voice broke but she plunged on bitterly. "I'd forgotten that you were at school together. But I had plenty of time to remember in that cell waiting for them to hang me."

"Deanna, you can't seriously believe—"

"Let go! I'm sick of your lies, your treachery! How it must have amused you to trap me as you did." A sob broke from her. "What a gullible fool I was."

"I sent no note."

The words, uttered with quiet desperation, hung in the air between them. She fell silent and looked at him. "What are you saying?"

"I know of no note."

She made a small sound of derision. "You were there, at the stable, exactly as your note said you would be."

"I was watching the inn. I saw you leave and followed you. You said we needed to speak privately. The stable seemed as good a place as any, but I had no idea why you were going there." Holding her by the shoulders, he said fiercely, "I did not betray you. But if I did, why would I come back to get you?"

Her eyes were resigned. Without shirking, she said, "Because not even the British could hang me without a trial first. The truth about you would have come out at it. They wouldn't risk that."

She had decided it to her own satisfaction, worked out all the answers, all the permutations. In her mind, he was the one already tried and found guilty. Still, he made one last attempt. "They could have tried you without witnesses."

Deanna shook her head. It had all come together for her in these last few minutes, the full realization of why Nash could not possibly have risked her going to trial. She should have seen it before and been prepared for what he had done.

"You're too valuable an agent to them. They couldn't take any risk of your being exposed." A sad smile touched her mouth. "People talk and when they do, they are frequently overheard. I, perhaps more than most, know that."

"It seems you know a great deal," Nash said. His voice was without emotion, his face expressionless. Later, he would deal with the pain ripping through him. But not just then. "Come."

She dug her heels into the ground, resisting. "There is no point. I will only keep trying to escape. Eventually, I'll succeed."

Nash looked at her for a long moment. Slowly, he nodded. "So be it."

Before she had a chance to realize what he was doing, he pulled a leather thong from his pocket and looped it around her wrists, securing it firmly.

"What do you think you're doing?" Deanna demanded, outraged.

"I'd say I'm living up to your expectations," Nash replied. Without a further word, he pulled her after him into the woods.

By midday, the sun had risen high in the sky and the air turned noticeably warm. Astride the horse Nash had put her on, Deanna struggled to maintain her balance despite having her hands bound and being without stirrups. He had removed them without comment before they started out. Their absence made it impossible for her to get away.

Thwarted at every turn, worn out in mind and body and more thoroughly confused than she had ever been, it was all Deanna could do to keep from weeping. She had always cried more easily than she liked, but this time she absolutely would not give in to it. She would die before giving him that satisfaction.

They had been riding for hours. Their direction was south, which puzzled her. She wouldn't put it past Nash to deliberately travel in a circle to keep her from guessing where they might be going.

It was on the tip of her tongue to ask him—as it had been since they set out—but she stopped herself. They could be on the road to Hades for all she knew, and she wouldn't say a word. Actually, *couldn't* would be a fairer description. Her throat was raw with unshed tears and her mouth painfully dry. In addition, she was hungry.

To her acute embarrassment, her stomach chose that moment to rumble loudly. Nash was riding directly ahead, holding her horse on a lead line. He glanced over his shoulder.

"We can stop if you like."

They were the first words he'd said to her in hours, and they were kindly uttered, which made them all the worse. Stubbornly, she shook her head.

He shrugged and continued on. But before they got more than a few yards, her stomach did it again.

Nash reined in and dismounted. He lifted her from the saddle, catching her as she staggered. "I thought you rode," he said accusingly.

"With stirrups," she shot back, "and with my hands free. You try it this way and see how well you do." Angrily, she tried to brush a stray lock of hair out of her eyes but couldn't manage it with her wrists bound.

Nash did it for her, his fingers lingering a moment against her skin. Catching himself, he abruptly pulled his hand away. "I will untie you on one condition."

She looked at him suspiciously. "What's that?"

"That you give me your word you will not try to escape in the next hour."

Deanna hesitated. She was struck by his apparent willingness to believe her, but torn between her desire to continue resisting and the practical realization that escape was at best a remote possibility.

She had no idea where she was, no food or weapons and little prospect of finding her way to safety, presuming there was any such thing. If she accepted his offer, she would at least have a chance to regain her strength and perhaps discover something about where they were and where they were going.

Reluctantly, she nodded. Nash's eyes held hers as he drew the knife from the scabbard on his leg and cut the leather thong. "See to your needs," he said curtly. "I'll get a fire going."

When she returned to the small clearing a few minutes later, the fire had been lit and a pot set over it. Good smells teased her. She accepted the wooden bowl he offered and tried not to look too eager as he filled it with a savory stew.

"I hadn't realized you cook."

"A friend provided this," he said without further explanation. They ate in silence for several minutes. Deanna finished first. Nash noticed and refilled her bowl. She nodded her thanks grudgingly and continued eating.

When they were done, he rose and began banking the fire. The hour he had allotted was almost over. Deanna felt a pang of regret. Despite the wall of betrayal that lay between them, there had been an odd sort of pleasure to sharing the simple meal.

She rose reluctantly as he approached and held out her hands. The thong he had tied earlier had left faint red tracings on her wrists. Seeing them, his face tightened.

"It would save us both a great deal of trouble if you would simply agree to come along peacefully."

Deanna debated within herself. The more time she had to think about it, the more she realized that escape was not the solution. Or at least it wouldn't be until she had some idea of where to escape to. Still, she was loath to simply give in to him. "Come along to where?"

He smiled, as though anticipating her response. "Virginia."

Chapter Thirty-Eight

"Virginia?" Deanna repeated dazedly. This made no sense. Virginia was the stronghold of the American forces. Washington's headquarters were there. It had to be a trick. "You wouldn't dare go to Virginia."

"Wouldn't I? There's only one way for you to find out."

"It would be suicide," she insisted. "Especially if I'm with you. You would—" She broke off and went pale.

Nash shook his head in disgust at her train of thought. "You've already been a fool," he said harshly. "Don't be a complete idiot."

Her suspicions embarrassed her, but she couldn't dismiss them entirely. How could he seriously contemplate walking right into the heart of the American forces accompanied by a woman who believed him to be a traitor?

Either he was lying about where they were going

or—or she was terribly wrong about him. "I don't understand," she said softly.

A rueful look of sympathy darted across his face. "That makes two of us, but at least we can try to make the best of it. Will you give up the idea of escape?"

Deanna thought quickly. Below Virginia were the Carolinas, still held by the British although in hot dispute. If they went too far south, she would find herself there instead.

But no alternative presented itself and finally, reluctantly, she said, "I cannot be sure how far we traveled last night but my guess is that we are somewhere west of the New Jersey Palisades."

His fleeting look of surprised approval told her she was right.

"From there," she continued, "it should take us no more than five days to reach Virginia."

"That presumes a brisk pace."

"Yes," she agreed, "it does. If we are not in Virginia by then, the truce between us ends. All right?"

He hesitated, clearly not pleased by the terms but at length he nodded. "I suppose it will have to be." Briskly, he strode over to where the horses were grazing. "Here," he said as he pulled stirrups from his saddlebag and attached them to her horse. "If we're going to keep to that schedule, you'd better be able to ride properly."

"I'll do my best," she murmured, and swung lightly into the saddle.

* * *

Four days later, Deanna had cause to regret her rash promise. Not that she was still thinking about escape. That was out of the question. She ached in every bone of her body, was chafed in places she'd never really thought about before, and had been bitten by what she was sure was a representative of every kind of insect in North America.

They had traveled by horse and by ferry, along the coast and along rivers, over hills and through marshes. They had been scoured by sun, soaked by rain and whipped by wind. The savory stew by the campfire had proven a fleeting thing. Their food consisted of dried deer meat, handfuls of nuts and whatever they could glean from the land.

By afternoon of the fourth day, she had begun to fantasize about long hot baths and scented shampoo, silk undergarments and toasty fires. Or just plain toast—that would be fine—spread with Martha's blackberry jam.

Her mouth watered. She stifled a sigh and attempted for perhaps the tenth time in the past hour to straighten her shoulders. It simply wouldn't do to let Nash see how terribly tired she was. He'd think he was winning.

Not that this was any sort of contest between them—certainly not. They were simply fellow travelers, thrown together by unlikely circumstances, to be sure, but nothing more.

Indeed, they hardly spoke as they rode along. And at night they went chastely to their own beds on opposite sides of the fire, within sight of each other, although she couldn't say she'd seen him looking whenever she did.

She didn't regret his aloofness, not even for a moment. What she had allowed to happen between them—twice no less—was inexcusable. Obviously, where he was concerned, she couldn't trust herself. Therefore, it was best to have as little contact with him as possible during this enforced journey... which did not explain why she was staring straight ahead at his back, watching the graceful play of muscles under the shirt he wore and admiring how very well he sat a horse.

Exasperated with herself, she looked away and did not notice that he had drawn rein until her horse almost walked into his. "Why have we stopped?" she asked.

Nash dismounted and began removing the tack. "It'll be dark in a few hours."

"We could keep going until then."

He uncinched the saddle and pulled it off. "I don't know about you, but I could use an early night. Also, I'd like a chance to get something to eat that a man can actually live on."

The thought of an early rest and a break to their monotonous diet delighted her, but she restrained her enthusiasm. "Oh, well, if you really feel you need to."

"I do," he said firmly. Before she realized what he intended, he reached up and lifted her from the horse. "And so do you, so stop pretending otherwise." He looked her up and down critically. "You look like a good puff of wind would knock you over."

Deliberately, she subjected him to the same scrutiny. "At least I don't look like a grizzly."

His eyes widened. "A what?"

"You heard me. A grizzly. You haven't shaved since we started out, your hair's down to your shoulders, and as for your choice of garb—" Her nose wrinkled.

Nash looked at her in wonder for a moment before he threw his head back and laughed. "How remiss of me. I didn't realize Your Ladyship was offended."

"I'm not. I'll have you know I used to go on fishing expeditions with my brothers that made this look like a picnic."

"You did, did you?"

She nodded. "All the time."

"Does that mean you can actually catch something?"

She looked at him scornfully, ignoring the rapid-fire beat of her heart. "Better than you, I'll bet."

"You're on. There's line and hooks in the pack. I'll get the horses settled. You find a couple of long green branches about like this." He showed her with his hands.

"I know what to look for. You worry about the horses." She glanced around. They were in a small clearing just off the trail. It looked as though it might have been used as a camp before. She caught a glimpse of water through the trees. "I'll meet you by that creek."

Nash joined her a few minutes later. She had waited to put her hook in until he could do the same. Fair was fair.

"Sure you want to fish from there?" she asked as he settled comfortably on the bank.

He shrugged. "Seems fine to me."

"Suit yourself." As for her, she had her eye on a spot a little downriver, out toward the middle where the water eddied in a way that suggested there might be a deep pool just a short cast off. The kind of place the big old grandpa trout liked to be.

With an innocent smile, she waded out. Her first cast was slightly off. Her second was better. It had been a long time since she'd fished but the fine art of it was coming back to her.

Nash didn't bother to recast. He left his line in the water and leaned back against a nearby tree. After a few minutes, his eyes drifted shut.

All the better. Maybe she'd be nice and let him share what she caught. A splash in the pool caught her eye. She moved forward eagerly, lifted her line to cast again and—

Her feet went out from under her. She lost her balance and fell, coming up wet and gasping. "Of all the damn—"

"Language, Deanna," Nash said from the bank. He had awakened and was watching her with evident amusement. "I'm shocked a lady of your bearing would indulge in any untoward conduct."

Considering that she looked anything but a lady just then, dressed in soaking wet breeches and a linen shirt that was turning alarmingly transparent, and considering that he had better reason than anyone to know exactly what sort of untoward conduct she was really capable of, she thought his comments tactless, to say the least.

Sputtering, she got to her feet and tried to recover her pole. But it had gone sailing down the river. As she watched, a large, succulent trout—ten pounds at least—leapt out of the water, in a perfect arc and landed with barely a ripple.

Gnashing her teeth in frustration, Deanna stomped up the bank. She wrapped her arms around herself, partly to ward off the chill that was fast seeping over her but also to preserve what little modesty she still had. "We might as well give this up. I must have frightened off any fish for miles around."

"What was that I just saw out there?"

"No one ever catches that kind. They know it, they just like to taunt us."

He looked at her bemusedly. "I never thought of fish as capable of that sort of sophisticated behavior."

"I assure you they are."

"It doesn't bother you, then, to eat something that's clearly more intelligent than most of us?"

"From the look of things, that won't be a problem today."

"Oh, I don't know..." Nash glanced at his line. The green branch bobbed, went still, bobbed again. "Excuse me," he said.

Moments later, he landed a glistening trout, large enough to feed them both well. "What was that?" he asked as they walked to the camp. "Something about beginner's luck?"

"Dumb luck," Deanna said. She shot him a quick glance. "You're no beginner."

"No," he replied softly to her back. "I'm not." With a grin, he followed after her.

Chapter Thirty-Nine

"Just one more bite?" Nash suggested. He held the spoon out. A tempting morsel of trout rested on it.

Deanna sighed. Wrapped snugly in a blanket Nash insisted she put on to ward off the chill she would otherwise undoubtedly take, she had found it almost impossible to feed herself. Not to worry. He had gallantly come to the rescue.

"I really shouldn't," she said, eyeing the fish greedily. Her appetites appalled her—all of them. Worse yet, he seemed fully aware of her weakness.

"It would be a shame to let it go to waste," he said. "You eat it."

"I'm full. Besides, I think I had more than my share already."

She resisted any temptation to engage in a discussion of what he had or hadn't had and swallowed the fish. Her stomach was happy, her body was warm, and she wasn't on a horse or a boat. She should have been blissfully happy. But all she could think of was Nash and how horribly, despicably nice he was being.

"Tomorrow's the fifth day," she said to remind them both.

"So it is."

"Are we in Virginia yet?"

"Almost."

"Horseshoes."

His eyebrows rose. "Pardon me?"

"Horseshoes. *Almost* only counts in horseshoes."

"Where did you hear that?"

"Somewhere, I forget. Anyway, it's true."

He got up to rinse his plate in a bucket of water near the fire. She watched him perform the ordinary task, thinking how very like him it was. To leave a plate unwashed might attract scavengers to the camp. He was a meticulously careful man who attended to details and seemed to leave little to chance. The kind of man a woman could count on.

And he was a blaze across the sun who had turned her life upside down and left her with a heart that seemed destined to ache forever. The kind of man a smart woman—which she obviously wasn't—would run from as fast as she could. It simply wasn't fair for any one man to embody such qualities. Not fair at all.

Her eyes felt weighted down by lead. She hardly knew it when Nash lifted her and carried her over to the soft bed of pine needles and blankets he had made. Moments later, he lay down beside her.

"This time," he said softly, "you sleep where you belong."

Deep in dreams already, she felt him draw her close against him and smiled.

* * *

His hand cupped her breast, the thumb rubbing lightly over her erect nipple. His manhood pressed against her buttocks. Slowly, he eased her over onto her back and moved the blanket that covered her.

He was naked, his body gleaming like polished bronze in the moonlight. Powerful and lithe, perfectly made, he came to her. Holding himself above her, he looked into her eyes. Gently, he said, "Are you awake, Deanna?"

She hesitated, tempted to let herself believe that this was a dream. It would be so much simpler if she could believe that. But the man above her was stunningly real. She could see the scar on his shoulder made by the newly healed wound. She could see other scars, as well, older ones, garnered over the years. He had been hurt, almost killed. He had bled and suffered pain. He had fought and struggled and survived. And he had brought her to a realization of her own womanhood that she would not have imagined possible.

"I'm awake," she said, soft on the night air, and met his gaze honestly.

"Touch me," he murmured. "I need your touch so much."

Her hand slid down him, tracing the contours of his chest, the flat, muscle-ridged abdomen and farther still, to the burgeoning strength of his manhood.

He moaned and closed his eyes against the waves of pleasure that she felt as surely as if they were her own.

"Tomorrow," he said as he bent his head and raked hot kisses down her breasts, "is the fifth day."

Tomorrow, when the sun began to tilt toward the west, their bargain would be over. But not now, not yet. Time could never be held at bay. All she could possibly do was store it up against the empty years ahead.

Her hands pressed against his shoulders. He let her push him down onto the bed and did not protest when she straddled him. Exultant freedom coursed through her. Emboldened as she had never been, she explored his body fully until his hoarse cry signalled that he could take little more.

He lifted her, holding her by the hips, and brought her onto him. But it was Deanna who joined them, encompassing him fully and bringing them both to shattering ecstasy.

They slept finally, limbs entwined, and did not stir until the pale shadow of the moon had yielded to the full blaze of day.

Neither spoke as they saddled the horses yet one more time and prepared to ride out. Deanna allowed herself only the barest glance at the little clearing. She swallowed hard, reminding herself that she had sworn to have no regrets. What had happened was of her own choosing. She could only pray the instincts born of the last few days had not been wrong.

They reached a hamlet shortly before noon. Pausing on a rise above it, Nash said, ''They've got a trading post here. We can pick up some things.''

Unspoken between them was the knowledge that the hamlet had a name. It belonged to a place. The question would be answered.

Slowly, Deanna followed him down the hill. Where the road widened slightly, a cluster of buildings stood. The largest appeared to be a tavern. Nearby was a small church that doubled as a school. Not far away was the trading post.

They left their horses hitched outside and entered. The place didn't appear much different from the general store in Belle Haven, a little rougher around the edges and not quite as well stocked but the same basic idea.

Deanna breathed in the familiar scents of tea and crackers, dried cod and pepper. Shelves held bolts of cloth, tins of every description, even a few precious books. A surprising indication of prosperity were the glass-enclosed display cases filled with patent medicines and gewgaws for the ladies. The war had raged through the entire area but this particular place— wherever exactly it happened to be—seemed to be surviving fairly well.

In fact, if she wasn't mistaken there was a dress hanging in the back that looked suspiciously like it could have come directly from Paris. Her eyes lingered on it. For all her claims to the contrary, she did like pretty clothes. Breeches were a pleasant novelty, but she wouldn't want to wear them forever.

Other, more important matters beckoned. As Nash headed toward the rear of the store, a plump woman bustled out from behind the counter. She gave Deanna a cautious smile.

"Morning, lad. What brings you to these parts?"

With her hair tucked up under the hat and the boy's frock coat on, Deanna wasn't really surprised to have her sex mistaken. But the moment she opened her mouth, the secret was out. "Just passing through."

The woman's eyes widened. She burst out laughing. "Darned if you didn't fool me. We don't get too many females coming by on their own."

"I'm not actually—" She glanced around. Nash was nowhere in sight. "Never mind. Could you...tell me something?"

"I can try."

"Where am I?"

"Why, shucks, honey, you're in King's Cross. Where did you think you were?"

King's Cross. Not precisely a common name, but there could have been a hundred of them scattered around the colonies. She took a breath. "Where's that?"

The woman looked surprised. She hadn't bargained on quite this level of ignorance. "How did you manage to get here if you got no idea where it is?"

"Dumb luck. Would you mind..."

Some measure of her desperation must have communicated itself. The woman's face softened. "Virginie, sweetheart. You're in God's own country, the sovereign state of Virginia. Hey, now what's the matter? You've gone all funny looking."

"I'm fine," Deanna assured her, although she was anything but. Torn between joy and shame, she felt as though she had just taken a hard physical blow to the stomach. "Excuse me," she said, and hurried for the door.

Chapter Forty

Nash turned from his perusal of the fancy dress and looked around for Deanna. She was nowhere to be seen. Frowning, he let the fragile material drop from between his fingers and went in search of her.

"Why, Mr. Nash," the plump woman said, spotting him, "I didn't know you were here." Her eyes turned suddenly shrewd. "You wouldn't happen to be with that pretty girl who was just in here, would you?"

"I sure hope I am, Nellie," he said. "Right now it seems a little up in the air. Where did she go?"

"Outside," Nellie replied with a chuckle. "She wasn't looking so good. Something about finding out she was in Virginia set her off."

Nash was halfway out the door before this last part was said. The horses were both still hitched to the post, a good sign. But where was Deanna?

She had been through so much in the past fortnight, more than many men he knew could have borne. And now she had to face the discovery that he hadn't lied to her.

If he could have found a better way to convince her, he would gladly have taken it. But she'd been adamant in her suspicions and, truth be told, he'd been too hurt to try to talk her out of it. Instead, he'd opted to show. Now, he had to wonder if that hadn't been too harsh.

The road in front of the trading post was deserted. It was a Saturday, he realized, so the school was empty. The neighborhood children would be off in the fields helping their parents. But the tavern never lacked for customers. Maybe someone there had seen her.

Three buckskinned woodsmen were enjoying a midday libation. They looked up sharply when Nash entered, relaxing when they saw who it was.

"Howdy, Nash," one of them said. "Come on over and sit a spell."

"I'd like to, Rand, but I've got a problem at the moment." Briefly, he told them what it was.

The men looked at each other in astonishment. "A filly? You gone and lost yourself a filly? Shoot, Nash, that don't sound like you."

"That's right," another said. "You got a certain reputation to uphold."

"This is different," Nash muttered. "Have you seen her or not?"

"Ain't seen nothing, specially not a girl dressed up like a boy running away from you."

This was apparently a knee slapper. Leaving the trio to enjoy themselves at his expense, Nash headed outside, his face grim. She had to be somewhere nearby, he guessed. Not even Deanna would be crazy enough to go off on foot. Maybe she'd just decided to take a look around. Except Nellie had said she wasn't looking so good.

Angrily, he berated himself for everything he'd put her through. If he'd tried harder, he could have found some way to spare her this. He'd just been so hurt and—

There, by the side of the trading post—was that a flash of golden hair he saw? It was, but very little else about Deanna was looking golden at the moment. She was wan and shaken, her eyes great pools of darkness. When she saw him, she took a quick step back.

"Nash."

He stopped, suddenly aware that he simply couldn't go barging up to her like this. He'd already done that far too many times. She needed gentler handling. Damn it, she deserved it.

"I was looking for you," he said, trying hard not to show how very anxious he had been. "Are you all right?"

She managed a weak smile. "Fine. Something I ate must not have agreed with me."

They'd eaten the same things for five solid days and nothing had bothered him. Or maybe it had. Standing there looking at her, he was starting to feel a little light-headed. "Come on back inside," he said, trying to urge her along without appearing to do so.

She came without an argument, something he took as a bad sign. The fight seemed to have gone out of her.

At the door to the trading post, she turned and looked at him. "Nash," she said softly, "I'm so terribly sorry."

But he was the one who felt repentant. Repentant for not having protected her better, for not having thrashed Charles to within an inch of his life while he had the chance, and for not being able to offer her what she truly deserved.

"Don't say that," he told her gruffly as he gathered her to him. There, on the porch in front of the store, smack in the middle of busy King's Cross, within sight of the three rogues peering from the tavern window and Nellie, smiling with delight, they embraced.

It was Nellie who finally drew them apart. She bustled over to the door, put her hands on her ample hips and said, "You don't let that child sit, she's gonna fall down."

Deanna laughed. She felt vastly better than she had, but there was no denying, her knees were weak. From the sheer emotion of it all, she told herself.

Nash led her inside and made sure she sat down. He leaned against the counter nearby, never taking his eyes from her.

"So what's the story?" Nellie demanded. Gossip good as this didn't come along too often. She wasn't about to miss out on the details.

"Miss Marlowe's a patriot," Nash said quietly. "Things got a little hot for her in New York so I'm taking her home."

This was news to Deanna. She had the distinct impression that Belle Haven was in the opposite direction. And besides, if things had been hot for her in New York, they'd be no better in General Tyron's Belle Haven. Sadly, she had to acknowledge that for her, going home was impossible, at least until this horrible war was over.

But none of that seemed to bother Nash. It took her a moment to understand why.

Nellie looked at him disapprovingly. "You still got that fellow, what's his name—Hargreave—working for you?"

Nash sighed. This appeared to be an old argument. "He's not such a bad sort, Nellie. You just never gave him much of a chance."

"No reason why I should. He's English."

"So am I, partly, and you put up with me."

Nellie laughed. "You know darn well why that is."

"I don't," Deanna chimed in. She thought it was past time for her to say something. Not a whole lot was making sense.

"Shucks, girl," Nellie said, "this here's just about the best damn—pardon me, darn—privateer in all of Virginie. Nash's boats been running the blockade since the war began. Ladies around here sure would be missing their fancy Brussels lace and the gentlemen would be running real low on brandy by now if it hadn't been for him.

"Not that that's all he brings in, or even mostly, but any time there's been just a little room left over in between the crates of guns and shot, he's squeezed in a few fripperies.''

"Actually," Nash said, "it's my captains who do that. They deserve the credit.''

"You were right out there with them," Nellie insisted, "least up till this past year, when you found something else to do.''

"What was that?'' Deanna asked faintly. Her mind reeled. Nash a privateer? Who was Hargreave? And above all, when was her stomach going to stop doing loop the loops and settle down again? Not any time soon, it seemed. At least not if Nellie had anything to say about it.

"He turned to spying," she pronounced. "Wasn't enough to be running the blockade. He had to go right in among the damn British, eye to eye with them, and trick them into giving up their secrets.''

"You're not supposed to know about that," Nash objected.

"Ah, heck, everybody around here knows about it. You may be a smart man, Edward Nash, but you got to realize, people talk. Speaking of which—'' She cast a shrewd look at them both. "You aren't seriously thinking of taking Miss Marlowe here home to that snooty Hargreave dressed the way she is?''

"Who's Hargreave?'' Deanna demanded.

"My butler," Nash murmured. He had the grace to look abashed.

"Your what?''

"Butler, honey," Nellie said. "But don't you worry none. You seem a right well-spoken young woman.

You just lay down the law to him first thing, make sure he understands who's in charge, and you won't have no trouble at all. I'm sure.''

"You have a butler?'' Deanna asked. Nellie's assurances notwithstanding, she was still stuck on that point.

"He used to be a butler,'' Nash said, hedging. "Now he more or less manages the estate for me while I'm gone.''

"The *estate?*''

Nellie let out a prolonged whoop. This was getting better and better. "Shucks, honey, Holycroft's more like one of them feudal manors used to be. Goes on absolutely forever. Why, you can't ride across it in less than a couple of days. But then you know that already, don't you?''

"Do I?'' Deanna asked faintly.

Nellie looked surprised. "You came down from New York, right? Well, then, you been on Holycroft land for at least the last day.''

"I inherited it from my mother,'' Nash said as though that somehow made it better. It didn't.

"About what she's wearing...'' Nellie bustled off to get the fancy dress, hanging up at the back of the store just like it had been waiting for Deanna.

Chapter Forty-One

The dress was exquisite. It was fashioned of white lace and silk and trimmed with tiny embroidered rosebuds down the skirt and bodice. The neckline was modest as such things went but the dress itself was so rigorously elegant and uncompromisingly feminine that only a confident woman could get away with wearing it.

Deanna had no choice. It was that or the buckskins, as Nellie was quick to remind.

"Think of this pretty thing as armor, child. You'll be a whole lot better off in it than in those boy's things you had on."

"I'm not sure about that," Deanna murmured.

"Why not?"

"I can't run as fast in this."

Nellie laughed. "Honey, the trick is not to have to run at all. Haven't you figured that out yet?"

"I'm working on it." Deanna glanced in the mirror Nellie had propped up on an old wooden trunk in the back room and said, "My hair's a mess."

The older woman grinned, rightly taking this as a sign of progress. "Don't you worry none. You wouldn't think it to look at me, but I used to be real good at fancy hair when I was down in Charleston."

"Were you a lady's maid?" Deanna asked in all innocence. How else would anyone gain experience doing hair?

"Heck, no. I worked in a whorehouse. One of the best in those parts."

"Really? How did you happen to come back here?"

"Now that's a real long story, honey. But fortunately, you got a lot of hair so maybe I'll just have time to tell you."

A half hour later, Nash returned from the tavern where he had sought a fortifying round or two and caught up on the news. The drink had been welcome, the news was not. Time was even shorter than he had thought.

The door to the back room was still securely shut but he could hear laughter coming from behind it.

Curious, he stepped closer in time to hear Deanna say, "No, not really? How did he ever get it out?"

"Brought up a tub of lard, they did," Nellie said. "Wasn't any other way."

Whatever they were talking about, it set off fresh gales of merriment. And prompted Nash to open the door. Immediately, both women broke off. They had the vaguely guilty air of having been up to something they shouldn't have been, but which they had enjoyed all the same.

Probably talking about men, he thought glumly. Women seemed to do that often enough. He suspected whatever they had had to say wasn't necessarily flattering. But any concern he had on that score vanished the moment he looked at Deanna. He quite simply stopped and stared.

He had always thought her lovely, never more so than those moments when she lay naked in his arms. But this was different. She was radiant, cool, womanly and extraordinarily beautiful all at once. The proud tilt of her head, the warm flash of her eyes and the perfection of face and form all combined to drive home to him how very special she really was.

And how swiftly their time together was slipping away.

Fiercely, he repressed that thought. It would be there to be dealt with later. But not now, not here. Not with her. "It's time to go," he said and held out his hand.

Holycroft glowed white in the setting sun. Riding toward it with Nash at her side, Deanna felt as though she was leaving one world and entering another. Behind her lay war and despair, turmoil and pain. Ahead lay only peace.

As Nellie had hinted, the house was a proud manor built in the Georgian style with two wings framing a center structure. Built of native stone, it rose nobly from the rolling lawns that surrounded it. Deanna had seen such houses before in England but never on this side of the ocean, although she had heard that they existed in such places as Virginia, where men held vast tracts of land and ruled like feudal barons.

Nash turned, and reaching across the distance that separated them, took her hand. Instantly, she responded, her body feeling the now familiar tingle of pleasure that happened whenever they came in contact and her spirit recognizing the even more profound bond that existed between them. A bond she could no longer deny, no matter what it cost her.

"Holycroft," Nash said, indicating the surrounding countryside with his free hand. "The borders stretch a day's ride in either direction. We had some fighting when the war began but it's since moved far off. You'll be safe here."

Deanna nodded but did not try to speak. She believed him explicitly yet she also noted what he had not said. *You'll* be safe, not *we'll*.

"Where is the fighting now?"

He hesitated, and she knew her guess had been right. In Nellie's store, she'd thought she saw something in his face, some piercing regret she couldn't identify then. Softly, he said, "Cornwallis was defeated in the Carolinas. He has marched on Yorktown. Apparently, he intends to make his stand there."

"I see..." Her throat was suddenly tight. The magnificent house lying before her shimmered behind a veil of tears.

"The British fleet sails to his aid," Nash went on. "Washington will need every man and every ship he can get."

She raised her head, proud against the gathering night. The long heritage of strength forged in her ancestry, the strength of Daniels' Neck and the heritage of Amelia, came to her relief. "Promise me one thing?" she asked.

"Anything." He meant it to the very core of his being. It was a pledge born of supreme confidence in this woman, confidence that she would never ask of him anything he could not give.

"Don't leave until morning." She laid his hand close against her heart.

Chapter Forty-Two

He was fire in her arms, driving strength and remorseless male hunger. Beneath him, around him, lost in his power, she quivered helplessly.

They lay in the high four-poster bed in the master suite, draped in embroidered curtains, wrapped in night, lost in each other. Deanna only dimly remembered arriving at the house, meeting the formidable Hargreave and listening as Nash gave instructions.

To give the butler credit, she remembered that he never flinched. Supper had been served on damask and china, lit by tall white candles in silver sticks, discretion and luxury in every tiny detail. She had hardly tasted the food but she presumed it had been excellent. The wine had glistened in crystal goblets. A fire had burned beneath the marble mantel. The huge bed had beckoned.

Nash had undressed her in front of the fire with exquisite care, slowly removing each fragile garment. He took his time despite the effort it clearly cost. His cheeks were flushed and his pewter eyes gleaming when at last she stood naked in front of him, garbed only in reflected flame and the heat of his desire.

It was her turn then, though her hands were shaking, to undo the stock at his throat, unlace the fine linen shirt and undo the buttons of his breeches. Before she could finish, his control snapped and he finished the job hastily.

The bed was beyond their reach. On the floor in front of the fire, cushioned by the thick Araby carpet, they claimed each other. Their coupling was swift and fierce, but brought only faint surcease.

Gathering Deanna to him, Nash carried her to the bed. With infinite care, he laid her across the damask sheets. Her body was rosied by his lovemaking and he stood back and looked at her. "I will remember this," he said, "all my life and beyond."

"And I," she whispered, her body arching, her nipples hard and aching, needing him desperately.

He came to her with fierce strength, consuming her, leaving no part of her untouched. She welcomed him, matching his passion with her own, wishing only for this night to continue forever.

His mouth worshipped her, his hands adored her. With all his body he paid homage to her womanhood. When at last they joined again it was a true union of their very souls.

Slumber claimed them, but even in its grip they held tight to one another. Nash slept on his side with Deanna curled into the arc of his body. One big hand laid possessively on her abdomen.

Barely had the first gray light of dawn begun to cast away the shadows of night than they woke to love again.

When at last they drew apart, neither sought sleep again. It was beyond them. Morning had come.

Servants brought buckets of hot water to fill the tub set in the dressing room. They entered through a separate door so Deanna did not see them, nor they her. But she could hear them going quietly about their task.

When they were done, she waited until she heard the water splash slightly. Rising, she walked naked into the dressing room.

Nash was stretched out in the tub. His eyebrows rose when he saw her. "Care to join me?"

The thought was tempting but she shook her head. "That doesn't look big enough." Indeed, the hard, burnished length of him completely filled the tub.

He sighed in resignation. "At least keep me company."

Forever, she wanted to say, but this was not the time. "I'll do better than that." She mustered a smile.

Nash groaned with pleasure as she scrubbed his back. She made a thorough job of it before going on to other things. A great deal of water splashed on the floor before they were done.

"I still say you look like a grizzly," she observed some time later.

Curled up in a chair near the tub, she watched him shave with unbridled fascination. At length, the week's worth of beard was gone and his square jaw once again revealed. "About the hair," she said.

They changed places. Still as naked as a jaybird, she fussed over him, brushing and trimming his hair until it was again contained in a neat queue at the back of his neck.

"You're very good at that."

Straight-faced, she said, "Nellie gave me some tips."

"I'll just bet she did." Nash reached for her. Too soon, he remembered himself. With palpable regret, he let her go. "I must dress."

She nodded, determined not to let him see her anguish. "I suppose I should do the same." She left him then and went back to the bedroom. The white lace and silk dress had been left on a chair. She put it on carefully and did her hair the way Nellie had showed her, so that soft curls framed her face.

She finished just as Nash emerged from the dressing room. He was garbed in black, the way she had first seen him, relieved only by the flash of his white stock. A sword was buckled around his lean waist. He looked equally well prepared for a fancy dress ball or a war.

That thought struck her as oddly touching. She went to him and laid her hand on his arm. Her voice was husky. "I want you to know I'm going to be good about this."

His gaze searched hers. "Are you?"

"Marlowe women are known for it. The British have nothing on our stiff upper lips."

"Actually, I find your upper lip delectable. Also the lower one."

She shut her eyes for a moment, calling on all the pride and courage she possessed. "Don't," she whispered, her only concession to the pain that threatened to wrench her apart.

They walked down the long, curving staircase together. Hargreave awaited them at the bottom. Deanna remembered him vaguely from the previous day. He was a slightly built man of medium height, and didn't look quite the ogre he had been painted.

"Miss Marlowe will be staying," Nash said.

Hargreave inclined his almost bald head. He did not look at Deanna. "Sir."

"She may wish to make some changes."

It was difficult to say who was the more startled, Hargreave or Deanna. As brief as her acquaintance with Holycroft had been, she had the distinct impression that it was perfect. She said as much.

Slowly, as though he hadn't much practice doing it, Hargreave smiled. "Thank you, miss."

Nash looked from one to the other, satisfied. "That will be all," he said.

Hargreave bowed. Softly, he said, "Godspeed, sir." With utmost discretion, he walked away, leaving them to share a final few minutes alone.

Deanna's lips were tender and full. She stood at the large window near the door, staring out. An immense black stallion had been brought from the stable. He snorted and pawed the ground but quieted when he saw Nash.

Once mounted, horse and man were one. Nash turned, looking toward the window and the woman framed there. Framed, too, by the great house all around her, the walls stretching out as though against eternity and the vast land rolling on forever heedless of the tides that swept across it.

She touched her fingers to her lips.

He put his heels to the stallion's sides and was gone.

Epilogue

Deanna slowly put down the letter from her father and stared into the fire. It was warm in the library of Holycroft, but outside the first chill winds of autumn were beginning to blow over the land. A silver tea service was on the table beside her, along with a bell for her to ring should she require anything. Anything at all, Hargreave had stressed.

He seemed to think it was his duty to look after her and make absolutely sure she did not exert herself. When he'd caught her the previous day laying a fire in the sitting room, it had been all she could do to calm him. Any hope of more ambitious endeavors was clearly out of the question.

She was left with her knitting, which she was slowly getting good at, her reading, which she genuinely enjoyed and sedate rides on a gentle mare. That and the letters that came frequently from her father, less so from Nash. But then her father was at Belle Haven, holding on as best he could, and vastly comforted to know that she was safe. Nash was in the thick of it, at the siege of Yorktown. Deanna prayed daily that a climactic victory there would end this terrible war.

Charles was dead. So her father had informed her. He had perished not gloriously or even to any purpose, but in a boating accident in New York harbor, the result apparently of a drunken excursion by officers who had nothing better to do.

Clinton had kept his forces in the city. Despite repeated orders from Cornwallis, he had yet to march to the relief of Yorktown. That decision, more than anything else, emboldened the Americans, who fought with the desperation of men who knew this might well be their only chance at victory.

Her father, who now knew the full story of her arrest and escape—or as full as propriety allowed—agreed with her that it was likely Charles had sent the letter that brought her to the stable. Nathaniel had noticed Charles, at the picnic in Greenwich Village, watching her and Nash as they emerged from the woods.

Nathaniel admitted a little wryly that he had wondered who the man she was talking with was and had thought about asking her, but before he could do so events had overtaken them. He seemed reconciled to the fact that his daughter's rescuer was a rebel American, as he also seemed to accept the possibility of British defeat.

"The hand of destiny," he wrote, "may yet decree that this vast, sprawling land is meant to be self-governed after all. Perhaps it would even be for the best."

Her brothers were home again and reconciled, but also determined to go their separate ways. As for Nathaniel, he was planning his return to England although he allowed as to how he might visit from time to time when, as he said, things had settled down. The thing he had most particularly in mind was Deanna's happiness, but he was gracious enough not to stress the point.

She spared a quick glance over her shoulder to be sure the library door was closed and stood up to poke the fire. After all those years of helping to look after Daniels' Neck, she couldn't simply sit back and do nothing.

When the fire leapt again, she tossed around for some other way to engage her restless energy. She could write to Nash, as she frequently did, but she couldn't be sure that in the chaos of an approaching battle he would have any chance of receiving the letter.

Besides, what concerned her most, apart from the immediate issue of his safety—the consuming fact that dominated her days—she would not write of at all. Nor would Hargreave or anyone else, for she had expressly forbidden it. Nash had far too much on his mind to worry about her. He needed to believe her safe, content and utterly without concern.

Would that it were true. She touched a hand lightly to her belly and smiled. If her calculations were correct, the life within her had begun that final night of their journey after they entered the borders of Holycroft. That seemed fitting somehow.

On an impulse, she left the library, and with a cloak thrown around her shoulders, wandered outside. Everywhere she looked, the vast demesne of Holycroft was being prepared for the winter ahead.

Bountiful crops had been brought in, provisions of every sort laid up, buildings repaired. There was no shirking of the slightest duty, but on every face and in every act was the knowledge that it might be for naught.

If Clinton did suddenly leave New York, if the British fleet proved as formidable as it always had been, if destiny simply willed otherwise, the whole great adventure of freedom would come crashing down around them all.

It did not bear thinking of, not here in the bright autumnal sunshine scented with the aromas of woodsmoke and apples, drying hams and corn cobs and the first faint whiff of approaching winter. Not here on the land of Holycroft, please heaven, where she walked with her child growing in her, and thought also of that other place, Daniels' Neck, the two now joined in her mind as one.

A brisk walk in the sunshine and a healthy dose of self-discipline kept her thoughts at bay, but only for a time. Too soon, shadows deepened and the lights began to go on one by one in the great house as night wreathed it.

Deanna ate a light supper served by Hargreave, who fussed over her with such solicitude that she was finally compelled to tell him she could not possibly take another bite. At his suggestion, she settled in the sitting room but declined the offer of coffee. Her nerves already felt painfully jangled.

Because the butler would not go to bed until she did so herself, she retired early, but sat up in bed trying to concentrate on the book she was reading. It was a good tale, all about love found, lost and found again. But she could not give it much heed.

Night sounds intruded through the window she had left open a notch—the hooting of owls, the flutter of wings, the whisper of the wind. They were mournful sounds that stirred her thoughts to melancholy and made her shiver in the bed.

In her mind's eye, the sounds transformed into the clash and fury of battle, the screams of dying men and horses, the bloodred mist of destiny hanging in the balance.

She woke with a start, unaware that she had slept, and sat up. The battle. It had been so real. She had smelled the powder and the iron tang of blood, been close enough to touch the frayed standards, waving above the advancing forces, lit by exploding shells as the fortifications were breached and—

This was madness. She could not possibly know of such things. It was only her imagination set at a devil's pace to torment her.

The bed that had been a comfort was turned suddenly treacherous. She could not trust herself to sleep again, not when such dreams lurked just around the corner of unconsciousness.

It was chill in the hallway but the robe she wore kept her warm enough. She knew, thanks to earlier noctural wanderings, that the fires would be banked in the kitchen. She could make herself a cup of warm milk.

But she had gotten only a little way, no farther than the central hall, when a new sound reached her through the night. Not hoot nor flutter nor breath of wind but the swift, sure pounding of—what? Horse's hooves, coming, coming, faster now over the land of Holycroft.

Deanna ran toward the door and wrenched it open. This, too, might be a dream, even more tormenting than the last. But she had to know, had to see for herself, had to pray that it might be—

The black stallion reared, dark against the night, silver hooves flashing beneath the moon. A deep voice murmured soothingly. The horse settled and was quiet as his rider dismounted.

He was limping. That was what she saw first and what pierced through her. Without thought, she ran to help him.

He stopped, gazing at her like a man long parched for water. His arms opened. On a wing, she went into them and was gathered close.

"*Nash* . . . I didn't dare hope. Your leg . . ."

"A nothing wound—but honorably gotten." There was a smile in his voice. He squeezed her again hard, then set her slightly aside so that he could look at her. His eyes gleamed, fierce and proud. "It is done." With a sudden, triumphant laugh, he repeated, "Done and well done, by God! Scarcely two days ago. I came as swiftly as I could."

He had crossed Virginia in two days, riding injured to reach her. She swallowed hard and did her utmost to look stern. "We must see to that *nothing* wound of yours before it becomes something more."

"Do your worst, sweetling," he said with a grin. He wrapped his arm around her and turned toward the house. Only then did he freeze, his eyes widening as he felt the slight thickening of what had been willow slim.

"Deanna?"

"Hmm?" Bursting with happiness, she tilted her head to the side and looked at him.

The corners of his mouth quirked. He gave a huge, masculine sigh. "It appears just as well I have been in correspondence with your father."

Not fair. She had been just about to gain the upper hand with her precious secret, and he seemed not at all astounded. Indeed, he appeared to take it in happy stride.

"My father..."

"He wrote to say he intended returning to England. I wrote back offering to buy Daniels' Neck."

"You did what?"

Nash looked at her with mock sternness. "Hear me out, woman. However, he also suggested that if I truly had a yen to divide my time between there and Holycroft, you were the person to discuss it with."

"I?"

"You," he affirmed, his hand sweeping over her belly with frank possessiveness. "He means to deed it to you."

Deanna's shoulders straightened. He could be the most infuriating man, always taking her by surprise. She would really have to put a stop to that if they were to deal well together. "I will never sell Daniels' Neck," she said.

He stroked a finger down her cheek and smiled when she trembled. "Then perhaps we can work out something else."

A sigh escaped her. Tomorrow she would begin the business of managing him better. Or perhaps the day after. He was home, that was all that counted. Time was theirs now. "Perhaps we can."

She was rewarded when he swept her into his arms, into love everlasting. Into the future.

* * * * *

Author's Note

   I hope you've enjoyed this second visit to Belle Haven and that you'll join me again for the third book of the Belle Haven saga, *The Tempting of Julia.*

   A century has passed since Deanna and Nash found each other in the midst of war. Belle Haven has changed from a quiet farming community to a retreat for the cream of New York society.

   But other, more enduring qualities have remained the same. For Deanna's great-granddaughter, Julia Nash, the challenge is still to find love in the midst of a world that too often seems to conspire against it.

   Belle Haven has become very real for me. I hope it has for you, too, and that you'll return there often.

Harlequin® Historical

WESTERN SKIES

This September, celebrate the coming of fall with four exciting
Westerns from Harlequin Historicals!

BLESSING by Debbi Bedford—A rollicking tale set in the madcap
mining town of Tin Cup, Colorado.

WINTER FIRE by Pat Tracy—The steamy story of a marshal
determined to reclaim his father's land.

FLY AWAY HOME by Mary McBride—A half-Apache rancher
rescues an Eastern woman fleeing from her past.

WAIT FOR THE SUNRISE by Cassandra Austin—Blinded by an
accident, a cowboy learns the meaning of courage—and love.

Four terrific romances full of the excitement and promise of
America's last frontier.

Look for them, wherever Harlequin Historicals are sold.

Take 4 bestselling love stories FREE

Plus get a FREE surprise gift!

Special Limited-time Offer

Mail to Harlequin Reader Service®

3010 Walden Avenue
P.O. Box 1867
Buffalo, N.Y. 14269-1867

YES! Please send me 4 free Harlequin Historical™ novels and my free surprise gift. Then send me 4 brand-new novels every month, which I will receive before they appear in bookstores. Bill me at the low price of $2.94 each plus 25¢ delivery and applicable sales tax, if any.* That's the complete price and—compared to the cover prices of $3.99 each—quite a bargain! I understand that accepting the books and gift places me under no obligation ever to buy any books. I can always return a shipment and cancel at any time. Even if I never buy another book from Harlequin, the 4 free books and the surprise gift are mine to keep forever.

247 BPA AJHV

Name _____ (PLEASE PRINT) _____

Address _____ Apt. No. _____

City _____ State _____ Zip _____

UHIS-93R   ©1990 Harlequin Enterprises Limited

Harlequin® Historical

HARLEQUIN HISTORICALS
ARE GETTING BIGGER!

This fall, Harlequin Historicals will bring you bigger books. Along with our traditional high-quality historicals, we will be including selected reissues of favorite titles, as well as longer originals.

Reissues from popular authors like Elizabeth Lowell, Veronica Sattler and Marianne Willman.

Originals like ACROSS TIME—an historical time-travel by Nina Beaumont, UNICORN BRIDE—a medieval tale by Claire Delacroix, and SUSPICION—a title by Judith McWilliams set during Regency times.

Leave it to Harlequin Historicals to deliver enduring love stories, larger-than-life characters, and history as you've never before experienced it.

And now, leave it to Harlequin Historicals, to deliver even more!

Look for *The Bargain* by Veronica Sattler in October, *Pieces of Sky* by Marianne Willman in November, and *Reckless Love* by Elizabeth Lowell in December.

HHEXP

Harlequin®Historical

THREE UNFORGETTABLE KNIGHTS . . .

First there was Ruarke, born leader and renowned warrior, who faced an altogether different field of battle when he took a willful wife, in KNIGHT DREAMS (HH#141, a September 1992 release). Then, brooding widower and heir Gareth was forced to choose between family duty and the only true love he's ever known, in KNIGHT'S LADY (HH#162, a February 1993 release). Now, Alexander, bold adventurer and breaker of many a maiden's heart, meets the one woman he can't lay claim to, in KNIGHT'S HONOR (HH#184, an August 1993 release), the dramatic conclusion of Suzanne Barclay's Sommerville Brothers trilogy.

If you're in need of a champion, let Harlequin Historicals take you back to the days when a knight in shining armor wasn't just a fantasy. Sir Ruarke, Sir Gareth and Sir Alex won't disappoint you!
